For Ruth, life in Africa is alive and beautiful...but, very lonely.

The mother elephant sucked up a trunkful of muddy, churning water and squirted a fountain at her baby. The baby, gleefully catching onto the game, shot a little fountain back at his mother. Soon the trees all along the edge of the pond were awash with spray. Bright, dancing drops fluttered between the sunlit leaves and through a hundred little rainbows, drenching Ruth to the skin as she clung like a terrified monkey to the huge old thorn tree.

The fountain sprays washed the red plains' earth off their backs, and they changed color before Ruth's very eyes until they were the brown of the earth up here in the hills. They frolicked together, as joyful and fresh as the morning sunshine, yet as ancient and as timeless as Africa itself.

Ruth's heart had stopped beating wildly, and she felt safer now as she watched them playing in the water. As she watched, she was entranced by the love between the mother and the child. An immense longing came over her—to be loved and to love with the same intimate joy. She longed to have it wash over her, immersing her with joy and life. But she shook the feeling away the instant it began to overwhelm her, and she focused her attention on the two creatures below her.

SALLY KRUEGER has seen much of the world. She was born in England and lived in Kenya as a child. She wrote *The Promise of Rain,* her first published work, while living in Scotland for a short time. Sally now lives with her husband and four children in Alberta, Canada.

The Promise
of Rain

Sally Krueger

Heartsong Presents

For Myles, a gift from God

A note from the author:
*I love to hear from my readers! You may write to me at
the following address:*   **Sally Krueger
                             Author Relations
                             P.O. Box 719
                             Uhrichsville, OH 44683**

ISBN 1-57748-253-0

THE PROMISE OF RAIN

Cover illustration by Jeanne Brandt.

PRINTED IN THE U.S.A.

one

1923
Kenya, Africa

Each day as Ruth fruitlessly scanned the horizon for some sign of rain, she let her eyes drift longingly downward to the jewel-green line of trees that filled the gorge as it cut down the hillside toward the valley just below the farm. Then, exhausted and hot after working all day in the sun's heat, she would make her lonely way through the dust and the long, dry grasses, squinting into the sun's relentless glare until she slipped into the cool, green light of the little valley. She had been coming often these days.

She made her way along the narrow pathway she had worn through the trees to the small, cold pool of water. Ruth slipped off her boots and began dangling her toes in the cool water when she felt her skin prickle with fear. Even before she saw them, she knew she was no longer alone. The weight of an ancient, primeval presence had silently settled on the valley, and the hair on the back of her neck stood on end. She was afraid to look up.

An agonizing moment later, she finally forced herself to face them. Ruth beheld an enormous cow elephant, with her calf proudly standing beside her. Their immense leather ears twitched and scanned for the slightest sound. Their trunks, one long and weatherbeaten, one small and supple, tasted and sniffed the cool air. A scent of danger spread itself like a mist throughout the little glade.

The elephants had emerged silently from the bush on the

5

opposite side of the pool. Ruth was paralyzed with fear, but they hadn't seen her yet, and she was downwind. She felt herself dwindle and shrink in their presence. The mother elephant took a step toward the water. Ruth knew she must get away.

There was an old thorn tree directly behind her, but the lowest branch was at least eight feet off the ground. As the cow turned to encourage her calf, Ruth saw her opportunity. She must not hesitate. Desperately, silently, Ruth jumped and reached for the branch, clawing painfully with her fingers until she was able to scramble up the trunk with her bare feet. She could hear the two elephants wading into the water behind her. Breathless with fear, she climbed as high as she could. At last she clung tightly to a thin branch while they filled their trunks with water from the pool directly underneath her.

She had never seen elephants in this valley before. They usually stuck to the plains below. But it was late in the dry season, and the streams down on the plain had become small, dirty trickles lost in the bottom of the wide, mud-cracked riverbeds. While precariously clinging to the tree, Ruth peered down through the branches at the two elephants.

The mother's great, gray legs stood like tree trunks growing out of the earth up toward Ruth's sanctuary above. Her ears, huge and delicate, flared outward, sensitive to each insect and every sound. Her trunk, as tenderly as any mother's arm, caressed her baby.

The mother elephant sucked up a trunkful of muddy, churning water and squirted a fountain at her baby. The baby, gleefully catching onto the game, shot a little fountain back at his mother. Soon the trees all along the edge of the pond were awash with spray. Bright, dancing drops fluttered between the sunlit leaves and through a hundred little rainbows, drenching Ruth to the skin as she clung like a terrified monkey to the huge old thorn tree.

If elephants could laugh, the whole of the small valley would be ringing with the sound, Ruth thought in spite of her fear. *Their laughter would rumble and peal, echoing all the way up into the hills above, filling all the earth with the awesome sound.* And here, so close to the source, Ruth ached with joy to hear it. Her own heart was so small and hard in comparison to the huge, free-living hearts of these great creatures, she was afraid it would shatter like glass just to be in their presence.

The fountain sprays washed the red plains' earth off their backs, and they changed color before Ruth's very eyes until they were the brown of the earth up here in the hills. They frolicked together, as joyful and fresh as the morning sunshine, yet as ancient and as timeless as Africa itself.

Ruth's heart had stopped beating wildly, and she felt safer now as she watched them playing in the water. As she watched, she was entranced by the love between the mother and the child. An immense longing came over her—to be loved and to love with the same intimate joy. She longed to have it wash over her, immersing her with joy and life. But she shook the feeling away the instant it began to overwhelm her, and she focused her attention on the two creatures below her.

The baby elephant noticed Ruth's boots on the edge of the water. He reached out with his trunk, picked one up, and tossed it high up into the air. Ruth watched it sail up past her head and crash down through some branches into the pond below. The little elephant bellowed with delight. He picked up Ruth's other boot and tossed it, too. Forgetting herself, Ruth laughed out loud, giving herself away. Suddenly everything became perfectly still. The mother sniffed the air with her trunk. Then as quickly and silently as they had come, the elephants withdrew, melting softly into the trees on the other side of the stream.

For a moment, the whole of the little valley was absolutely silent. Ruth held her breath. She was still afraid, yet she savored the sensation, like a mouthful of bittersweet liquid to quench an old thirst. For a few minutes, she had actually been alive with the terror and the joy. Quietly, she waited along with the rest of the valley to see if they returned; but there was only silence.

Then cautiously and slowly, the stream and valley began to stir again. After one or two tentative chirps, the chorus of birds resumed their musical banter. The muddy water swirled slowly around, settling the mud back into place until it ran clear and clean once more.

Ruth climbed stiffly down from her tree, noting all the scratches and bruises she had sustained in her flight upward. She stood barefoot on the rock overhang, peering into the middle of the pool to see if she could see her boots.

The presence of the elephant still lingered down here. It still flowed in the tumbling stream and hovered over the waters of the still, clear pool, a memory of joy. Ruth waded into the water to retrieve her soggy, mud-laden boots. The water was clear and shockingly cold. She felt the gentle current moving under the surface of the pond. Her boots were already covered in the settling silt. She picked them up, held them against her khaki shirt, and waded out of the water on the far side of the pool—the side from which the elephants had come and gone. Ruth looked both ways, and then she slowly made her way up the other side of the valley, her bare feet tender and bruised on the forest floor, her eyes watching for snakes that lurked in the undergrowth.

At the top of the valley, Ruth came out onto the dirt cart track that followed the little valley up the hillside to the lone farmhouse where Ruth was headed. Although the sun was low on the distant hills in the west, heat waves still radiated upward, stirred up by a scavenger wind, blowing hot over the arid landscape and devouring every green and living thing in its path. Ruth pulled out a crumpled khaki hat from her pocket and put it on. She plastered it low over her short, curly red hair and covered her green eyes and freckled cheeks, hiding them as best she could from the relentless sun and wind. She walked with long, lanky strides, picking her way over the burning dust of the road. Her wet khaki trousers and shirt whipped against her tall, lean body. She cut a lonely figure.

The farmhouse looked down on her from the hillside above. Its corrugated iron roof glinted a hard welcome in the sun. She didn't look up, but she knew her father was sitting on the veranda by now, waiting for the day to end. It was he who had forged this farm out of the stone heart of Africa forty years before. There were no other settlers in the area, and he was alone on the hillside, except for the Africans who belonged to the landscape and blended in with it the way he never would. Yet, over the decades, Africa had weathered and worn away at him, even as he had tried to shape it. Now he sat watching, like an old and gnarled anthill, long since abandoned, but not yet ground back to dust. Except for Ruth, he was still alone.

Her mother had come to Africa from Scotland along with her family, the Campbells, a fierce, resolute clan that had founded the town of Campbellburgh on the plains below Jack Jones's farm.

Morag Campbell was a delicate, gentle woman, and no one knew what she had seen in Jack Jones. In any case, she didn't last very long up here on the farm. She had died of typhoid fever when Ruth was only five years old. People said it was Africa that had killed her. Ruth treasured the few gentle, faded memories of her mother that she had hidden in her heart. What a difference it would have made to her life had Morag lived. Life with Jack had been hard and tough.

Even at this distance, she could feel his eyes on her as she made her way up the hillside. He was always watching, always squinting into the sun. She still didn't look up, but she knew where he was, sitting on the veranda under the bougainvillaea.

Jack had withdrawn into himself after Morag had died. It had made him harder and surlier than he already was. Ruth had been left to fend for herself. But he had taught her to farm, and these days she ran the farm almost single-handedly while her father watched from the veranda. It was hard work, and they would never be rich, the farm being so far into the hills as it was. It was too high and too remote, but Jack had intended it that way. He saw freedom in the isolation. And as he had predicted, the valley below had become riddled with settlers as well as with trophy hunters and tourists.

For Ruth, the isolation of the farm was her bondage. As she drew closer to the little house, the joy and lightness that had filled her while she watched the elephants seeped out into the dusty road and the parched grass. She trudged slowly up the hill, feeling as tired and empty as the cloudless afternoon sky hanging heavily above her. Her eyes were tired of searching, but still she scanned the distant horizon for the boiling thunderheads that signaled the beginning of the rains.

She climbed a wooden fence and made her way through the boma, its dry, scorched grass scratching at her ankles. The sun was starting to sink toward the hills on the far side of the valley now. Ruth could tell from the way it shone onto her back. It had weakened suddenly, the way the sun does in the tropics; and the wind, without its fierce accomplice, was beginning to hesitate and falter.

Ruth vaulted the fence on the other side of the boma and made her way across some patchy, scrubby grass that served as a front lawn. She had never much bothered with the finer points of gardening, except for the huge bougainvillaea vine that grew along the veranda. Her mother had planted it before Ruth was born, and Ruth always took great care to see that it was properly watered and trained. It was her one beautiful possession, the only thing she had ever had simply because it was beautiful, left to her by her mother, and she treasured it. Ruth glanced protectively over it as she walked gingerly over the spiky grass. It arched, blooming profusely with red-tissue petals all across the mantel of the veranda, and Ruth looked past it for her father. His chair was empty. He must have gone inside to refill his glass.

She hurried up to the veranda and put her boots to dry on the steps in the evening sun. She heard the front door open just as she scurried around the side of the house and slipped through the kitchen door. A burst of steam escaped as she went in, and she closed the door carefully behind her while her eyes adjusted to the muted indoor light.

"Jambo, Memsahib!" came the warm greeting from Milka, the cook. She and Ruth spoke in Swahili. "How are you? Here is your cup of tea." Milka pushed a tray with a teapot and cup across the table that stood in the middle of the kitchen, and Ruth pulled up a chair and sat down.

She poured out her tea and watched Milka bustling about the kitchen. Her white apron, always perfectly ironed and clean, and her crisp blue cotton dress underneath stood in stark contrast to her gently wrinkled, broadly cheerful face. Pots sputtered busily on the huge wood stove that stood in one corner. In the other corner sat a little toto, dutifully peeling potatoes. Milka chattered busily to him, scolding him and hurrying him along. Ruth sipped her tea quietly, as she did every evening, watching Milka get supper ready.

For Milka, the preparation of the evening meal was a task fraught with excitement and energy far in excess of its everyday regularity. Ruth always wondered how she made everything, no matter how ordinary, into a thrilling adventure. She had such untiring enthusiasm for living. Drained and empty, Ruth slouched with her elbows on the table, watching Milka whip up some eggs for the Yorkshire pudding. Fat sizzled fiercely in the oven and water for the potatoes boiled rapidly on the stove. The very air crackled with energy as it swirled and eddied around Milka as she worked.

Milka brought a religious fervor to her work. Having been at the mission school for one year when she was a girl, Milka had proudly embraced the Christian faith and considered her place in the Joneses' home to be God's personal calling to her. It was Milka's deepest sorrow, she'd told Ruth, that Jack had never allowed his daughter to attend church. Milka, with true Christian zeal, had tried unsuccessfully to instill something of her faith in Ruth's life. Over the years, Ruth had grown accustomed to hearing Milka's constant assurance of her prayers. If Milka had ever become discouraged, Ruth would have had to admit that she would genuinely miss them. In a strange, disbelieving way, Ruth had grown dependent on Milka's prayers for her.

She had been their cook since Ruth was born. In fact, she had been trained by Morag, which was quite unusual because most cooks were men. Milka had never ceased to take her unique position as cook, as well as her unofficial position as mother to the lonely little girl who grew up here on the farm, with the utmost seriousness.

Milka whisked a mug out of the cupboard and poured herself some tea. The Yorkshire pudding was in the oven, the potatoes were peeled, and the long-suffering toto was washing bowls and pots. "How was your day, *Memsahib*?" she asked, sitting down opposite Ruth with one eye on the toto and the other on the potatoes. When Ruth told her about the elephants, Milka's eyes grew wide with horror.

"*Memsahib,* you must be more careful! They could have

trampled you to death. Lord have mercy! He must have had His angels watching for you today, *'Sahib!'*

Ruth laughed at Milka's concern for her, but then she grew more thoughtful.

"You know, Milka, when I saw such magnificent, gentle, fearsome beasts as I hung up there in that tree this afternoon, I couldn't help thinking that they must indeed be a work of God. So much power, and yet what loving-kindness perfectly blended into one creature."

"Well, praise be to God above!" said Milka, lifting her eyes dramatically to the ceiling, where the steam from the boiling pots was collecting like a pillar of cloud. "He has given you a sign at last. My prayers will soon be answered. I am certain of it."

Now it was Ruth's turn to roll her eyes heavenward, and she laughed. This was not the first time Milka had received signs from God; and Ruth, as always, responded with good-natured skepticism. She even found herself wishing for a trusting faith like Milka's now and then. Wouldn't life be so easy? she patronized. Out loud she laughed and said, "Well, Milka, if the elephants are a sign from God, I for one certainly have no idea what He could possibly mean by them. He will have to be more explicit, thank you very much."

"Ah, but God moves most mysteriously," countered Milka, her eyes twinkling with the challenge. This was her favorite type of discussion. "You can never tell what He is going to do, but He is up to something, you mark my words." She spoke in solemn and dramatic tones.

Ruth shook her head and put her empty teacup down on the table. Usually she would tease Milka about a God who would give people signs from heaven whose meanings were impossible to understand. Surely, if He were truly God, she would say, He would be capable of making Himself clear. And Milka would exclaim passionately that He did indeed make himself clear for those who had eyes to see and ears to hear. But today Ruth didn't argue or tease, she just pushed her chair away from the table.

"I'd better go and wash for supper," she said. Ruth had an odd flicker of feeling that God might, indeed, be stooping to touch her life after all these years. But the flame was too tiny and uncertain to talk about to anyone just yet, even Milka. She went out through the door that led down the hall to her bedroom. The house was quiet and cold. Night was moving in quickly.

Dinner was served formally in the dining room, a ritual left over from Morag's time and kept in perfect obedience by Milka. Even Jack dared not usurp Milka's authority on this issue. Ruth sat in her usual place at the long mahogany table, under the glare of the huge lion's head that hung on the opposite wall. Its glassy eyes, flickering sinisterly in the light of the hurricane lamp, glowered down at her as they had every night since she could remember. All along the other walls were the heads of antelope of all kinds, leering hungrily, yet unable to eat, like guests at a macabre banquet. Ruth shuddered and glanced quickly up into the rafters above, where, contrary to the natural laws, darkness seemed to overcome light, and the hurricane lamp shivered with fear even in the stillness. Supper was always served just after sundown. Ruth cringed, awaiting her father's entrance.

She heard him coming. He slammed the veranda door behind him. His footsteps echoed emptily across the hardwood floor of the lounge. The door burst open and Jack's presence filled the room. He was still a powerful man. He prowled unsteadily to the head of the table, sat under the mounted head of the lion, and glowered menacingly at the joint of beef in front of him. You could still see the vestiges of his youth, although his full head of once-black hair was now gray. He had a huge mustache, still as black as it ever was. Jack was a big man, although a lifetime of hard work had left him stooped and tired.

Milka came in from the kitchen and bustled about, serving the supper dishes. Ruth waited until she was finished.

"There were elephants down at the valley today," she ventured. "Only two, a cow and her calf. It was a close call, but I managed to get up a thorn tree before they saw me."

"Well, I'll have to go and shoot them if they come any closer or they'll get into the coffee." Jack dug into the roast beef and the boiled potatoes. "Which way were they headed?"

"I didn't see," Ruth answered shortly. Jack didn't reply.

"Are you going to Angus Campbell's funeral tomorrow?" She tried another tack.

"Humph!" came the reply. "I'd sooner stick my head in the jaws of a crocodile than go anywhere near that Campbell woman." He stuck another forkful of meat into his mouth.

"Besides, she's called some sort of landowners' meeting for the day after her own husband's funeral, and she can't expect me to go scurrying back and forth into town every day of the week. I have better things to do. Go yourself."

It was Ruth's turn not to reply. She wondered what kind of meeting Florence would be calling so quickly after her husband's funeral. But it was the funeral that concerned Ruth most. She loathed social occasions of every kind. She hated being stared at because of her old-fashioned, badly fitting clothes that once belonged to her mother. She hated being too timid to talk to anyone. On the rare occasions when someone did speak to her, she usually managed to say something completely inappropriate in reply. But Florence would be expecting her, and Ruth was too afraid of Florence to risk her wrath.

Angus Campbell was her mother's brother and the son of old Hamish Campbell, the founder of Campbellburgh. Angus had finally died after a long, drawn-out illness whose actual nature had never been diagnosed. Upon hearing the news, Jack had growled that Florence had hounded him to death. Any man would have died after thirty years of marriage to her—it was a miracle he had survived that long!

Ruth couldn't help but think Jack was probably partly right. Florence was indeed a fearsome woman, and everyone in Campbellburgh lived in terror of her tongue and her temper. Everyone except Jack Jones. Unfortunately for Ruth, Florence had developed a special interest in her upon the death of her sister-in-law and had taken it upon herself to see to her niece's proper Christian upbringing. Every month or so, she arrived in her surrey and descended upon the little farmhouse like a battleship putting into a humble fishing village. Ruth, who had been notified by toto of her impending visit, would stand on the veranda to receive her, while Jack rumbled and grumbled in the background.

Florence would sail up the veranda steps armed with a large, folded sunshade held lance-like under one arm and an incongruously dainty handbag in the other. Her fiercely feathered hat set off her flashing eyes and the determined set of her chin. She was still a very handsome woman, but only, in Ruth's opinion, if one were able to look past the warlike character that radiated around her. Her ample bosom was swathed in silk, and her skirts rustled richly as she bore down on Ruth for the kiss. Ruth braced herself and endured the onslaught of perfume that stung her eyes like gun smoke.

When it was over, Florence would turn on Milka, who had been standing by unobtrusively, and demand tea. Milka would shoot her a sullen glare and angrily scuttle off while Jack emerged from the lounge. The two old generals would glare at each other for a moment, confirming the tense truce between them. Then Florence would sail into the lounge with Ruth meekly in tow. This scene was as familiar as old curtains to Ruth.

Sometimes Florence brought along Annie, her pretty daughter, as an example to Ruth of proper, ladylike refinement. Over the years, Annie and Ruth had developed a genuine friendship through these visits. Annie possessed a bubbling joy that Ruth envied with all her heart. It was the joy that made her as beautiful as she was. She actually looked very much like her cousin Ruth; but where Ruth was tall, Annie was willowy; and where Ruth moved clumsily, Annie was graceful; and where Ruth had carrot-red hair, Annie's hair was a delicate strawberry blond.

Ruth wondered how Annie was now that her father had died. She had idolized him, and she must be suffering deeply. Ruth wished there were something she could do for Annie. As she looked over at her own father finishing his plate of supper under the protective glare of his lion's head, she knew she, in her powerless and helpless state, would never have anything to offer her cousin. She knew that even in her grief, Annie would be drawing on reserves of her secret store of joy to see her through. The silence at the table was becoming oppressive.

Ruth pushed her plate away. "Excuse me, Father. I need to get to bed early tonight since I will be going into town for the funeral tomorrow."

Jack grunted as he disposed of another forkful of supper.

Ruth slipped off to her bedroom. She put on the cotton men's pajamas that she wore to bed and went to sit in her chair by the window as she always did in the evening before going to sleep. The loneliness crept through her like the dangerous darkness of the African night. The window was open, and she looked desperately outside to the night; but there was no help for her there.

The big thorn tree rustled mysteriously, and insects noisily went about their night's work in its leaves. The air outside wafted gently inside, carrying the scent of distant smoke and evening flowers all mingled. Silver-lined shadows flickered on the grass. There was a carpet of softly glowing stars miles and miles above the dark rafters of the house where freedom roamed, alive and vibrant, all across the African night. Far down in the valley, the sound of an elephant trumpeting rolled up into the hills above. An old, old memory somewhere inside Ruth stirred again, the way it had this afternoon as she watched the elephants playing.

She thought for an instant that someone was calling her name; only whoever it was, was still too far away to hear clearly. She strained her eyes to make out the dark shapes of the hills far across the plain, and the echo of the elephant trumpeting faded far away into them. The African night wrapped around her in unfathomable mystery as she got up and went to bed.

two

Ruth bumped along the cart track in the morning heat. She sweltered and seethed in the black cotton dress that had once been her mother's. Her mother had been a smaller woman than she was, and Ruth had to sit tall and rigid on account of the tight dress. She hung her head, despite the straightness of her posture, as though the weight of the wide-brimmed straw hat were too much for her to bear. In reality, it was the worry of her impending encounter with her aunt that bore down on her in the relentless sunshine.

The road to town wound down the hill to the little stream valley, joining it just below the pond where Ruth had seen the elephants yesterday. At the bottom of the hill, the road straightened out, stretching businesslike across the flat plain of the Rift Valley and making a beeline for Campbellburgh, whose red tile roofs sparkled proudly in the distance. The town was situated on a lake, just at the mouth of a lazy, winding river. Ruth looked over to where a cool, green belt of trees meandered along to the left of the road as the river headed slowly for town.

It was hot out in the open. Even the little clusters of African women, walking alongside the dusty road with huge baskets of vegetables on their heads, seemed cooler and more comfortable than she was. They wore long, loose clothes that captured every hint of a breeze. Their beads jangled from their ears and around their necks in gay, carefree colors. Ruth stared at them enviously, feeling hotter and more miserable with each look.

She passed a massive baobab tree standing alone in the

19

middle of the plain. Its enormous trunk bulged and bubbled like a giant carbuncle on the face of the earth. Ruth had always hated the old baobab. It was so out of place among the stately thorn trees whose graceful flat-topped branches so beautifully echoed the straight lines of the plains around them. But she could never bring herself not to stare at the baobab as she passed by. It always reminded her how little she fit into the life of the town of Campbellburgh.

Lately, a flock of slate-gray guinea fowl had taken up residence in the grass near the old tree. When Ruth passed by, they scurried off, cackling indignantly into the protection of the bulging trunk, and she was forced into a smile in spite of her bitter mood.

Ruth approached the town slowly. Dust from the wide streets rose into the air, and the whitewashed walls looked as though heat were dripping and rolling off them. The streets were full of people of all shades and hues. White settlers marched stiffly along the covered boardwalks in front of the shops. The men wore light suits and pith helmets, while the women floated gently alongside in soft, filmy dresses and wide, whimsical hats. Out on the dusty street, stately African ladies strolled along with huge baskets on their heads; while men lurked against posts, catching up on the latest news. Totos scurried in and out, darting past buggies and carriages that were heading, like Ruth, toward the church whose spire rose right up from the dead center of town.

Ruth was, indeed, a strange sight as she arrived at the church with the other mourners. Many of the townspeople of Campbellburgh were related to Angus and were arriving in droves, flocking into the gray stone church from all directions. As they passed by Ruth hitching her horse to the post, they smiled politely, if they noticed her at all, and went inside in muted little groups. Ruth stood by and watched them for a moment. She knew almost all of them by sight, as she was related in one way or another through her mother to many. They were a dour, sober lot, and they wasted no words on miscellaneous chatter. Watching them pass by her, she felt more acutely alone than she ever did up on the farm.

She looked furtively about for Florence, then realized she would be inside already. She breathed a sigh of relief and headed up the steps to the huge wooden church doors along with the rest of the townsfolk.

Ruth slipped into an empty pew near the back. She tried to make herself as small and inconspicuous as possible.

The church was filling fast, and Ruth's pew was becoming crowded. John Cooper, the town lawyer, and his wife, Mabel, squeezed down to Ruth's end of the pew. They nodded politely to her. Ruth nodded timidly back. John was a very large man, and Ruth found herself tightly pinned in the corner of the pew, pressed up against the wall. *At least no one can see me here,* she thought. She set her face like flint, grimly determined to endure the service and leave as quickly as she could.

The organist had been playing softly as the people entered. Suddenly the music roared loudly to begin the funeral. Florence sat regally in the front pew; but Annie, who sat beside her, looked shaken. Her heart went out to her friend, and she tried to send her a sympathetic smile, but she was too tightly jammed against the wall to be seen. The organ music suddenly ceased, and the reverend took up where it left off with his own funereal tone. Angus Campbell was the wealthiest, most influential person in town, and he would therefore need to be buried accordingly.

The church was hot and full, and it was not long before Ruth began to feel distinctly uncomfortable. John Cooper seemed to have inexplicably expanded, and Ruth's tight corner between him and the wall was shrinking considerably. The air inside the little church thickened and congealed like bland gravy so that Ruth found herself gasping and gagging, trying to get enough of it into her lungs. Still the Reverend Montgomery droned on and on. Women began to pull out fans and flutter them in front of their faces. Children were fidgeting, and the smaller ones began to whine. The men began to sink and slump into their starched shirts, coughing ominously like lions in the night. And still the air thickened and still the reverend droned.

Ruth was convinced Mr. Cooper was now twice his original size and sweating like a bull. Her stomach began to rise in protest, and the once orderly, straight rows of pews in front of her waved sickeningly before her eyes. Her ugly dress grew tighter and more uncomfortable with each breath she took. She knew she would never be able to stand to negotiate a path around Mr. Cooper in the state she was in, yet it would be dangerous to stay put. Panic gripped her like a cold claw. She was trapped. But it was the cold panic that saved her. She straightened up and faced the front. Only the most intense effort of will kept her from being ill. Mercifully, the Reverend Montgomery finally wound down like an off-speed gramophone, and there was a palpable sigh of relief from the entire congregation.

Florence and Annie Campbell sailed past as the coffin was borne out, and then everyone slowly oozed out into the aisle. Ruth stood up unsteadily. The wait for her pew to empty seemed interminable. But at last it was their turn, and Mr. Cooper shrank back to size and moved away. Ruth could hardly wait to breathe fresh air again.

Slowly the crowd rolled forward. But Ruth's relief was short-lived. Even in the aisle, she couldn't see anything past Mr. Cooper. The wait became unbearable, and Ruth began to gasp for air again. It was turning out to be much more diffi-cult to stand than it had been to sit. She felt the blood drain from her face, and Mr. Cooper's black coat took on a strange movement of its own, as if he had suddenly taken to doing some new kind of dance.

By the time Ruth and the last of the crowd reached the churchyard, the Reverend Montgomery was already speaking. The afternoon sun was beating down on her black dress. There was not a breath of wind.

Ruth could feel the sweat gathering under her dress and along her brow. The churchyard began to spin dangerously, and she knew she had better find some shade. The slow, stately river that had traveled beside her into town ran along below the church. Ruth slipped out of the churchyard gate and made for the line of trees along the riverbank. She leaned for a moment against the trunk of the nearest one. She was hot and sick, and she must somehow cool down. Spying the river glinting through the undergrowth, she found a little path and followed it down to cool her face in the water.

Standing precariously on a rock, she hiked up her skirts and reached down for a handful of water. There was a sickening rip and a sudden loosening of the dress around her waist. She stood up quickly and found a gaping tear all the way from under her arm to the small of her back.

"Oh, no!" she groaned out loud. Quickly she pulled the dress together and held her arm firmly over the ripped black material. Just then the branches behind her rustled, and out of them onto the bank stepped a stranger. He was tall, with windblown sandy hair. Ruth stared at him in horror. As he smiled kindly at her, and she was struck by the brilliant blueness of his eyes.

"Are you alright, ma'am?" he asked.

Ruth opened her mouth, but there were no words. She wanted to get away before he noticed her dress. Her right arm was clamped firmly to her side, holding her dress together. She stared past him to the path she must take to get back to the churchyard.

"Yes, I'm fine, thank you," she stammered at last, and she fled past him and up the path through the bush. Heat from embarrassment burned up inside her. Palm leaves whipped across her face like razors as she rushed through the undergrowth.

Finally she pushed her way onto the grassy lawn of the churchyard. Townspeople were just beginning to mill about, so the service was over at last. She furtively looked about for Florence and Annie among the mourners. She still had to offer them her condolences before she could escape.

She caught sight of Annie standing near her mother and chatting quietly with a group of her friends. Even in her grief, she was the image of perfect beauty, with her wavy blond hair, her fair skin, and sky blue eyes. Her navy blue dress gracefully swept down to her ankles. She looked cool and crisp, and Ruth stared enviously at her as she fearfully clutched her own dress.

One or two of the more eligible young men in town were standing watchfully near Annie. Ruth smiled ruefully. Annie had always led a train of captive hearts in her wake, but the man who managed to pass the muster of Aunt Florence and actually marry Annie would be a lucky man indeed.

She caught sight of Jimmy MacRae standing just outside the circle watching Annie. Poor Jimmy, Ruth thought, he must have fallen for Annie as well. Surely he knew that he didn't stand a chance. Florence would skin him alive if she even so much as caught a hint of those feelings. Ruth felt sorry for him. She liked him, even the little of what she knew of him. He had always spoken kindly to her when they met delivering milk at the train. But he was poor and he came from a poor family. The MacRaes had not settled on a very good piece of land, and they had always had trouble with one thing and another not going their way. It was just bad luck for the most part. But the wealthier farmers in the area had always looked down on the MacRaes, and Florence had been the leading figure in the campaign. Poor Jimmy MacRae.

She saw Annie smile over at him. She was always such a sweet person, Ruth thought. Just then Annie caught sight of Ruth watching her. She waved and called her over. Ruth smiled and hesitated, her right arm pressed stiffly against her torn dress. Soon everyone would see. She was sure Annie's friends were smiling condescendingly at her, and she hated it. She smiled tightly as she met their gazes. Annie stepped away from them.

"Oh, Ruthie, my dear, it's so nice to see you!" She put her arms around Ruth and hugged her. Ruth stiffly hugged back with her free arm, but she was grateful for Annie's greeting.

"Annie, I'm so sorry about Uncle Angus," Ruth whispered in her ear.

"Thank you. It was kind of you to come. I will miss him terribly." A shadow of sorrow fell across Annie's face, but Ruth thought that strangely it suited her. She looked more womanly, and there was a depth of feeling to her voice that Ruth hadn't heard before. "I don't honestly know how I will manage without him." She spoke the last in a whisper. Ruth thought Annie was about to cry, but suddenly she pulled herself together. "Anyway, it was awfully good of you to come, Ruthie." She smiled bravely.

"Aha, Ruth! I see you did come." The shrill voice of Florence Campbell pierced their conversation and they turned to face her. She strode toward Ruth, who had the sudden sensation of a cornered animal.

"I. . .I'm. . ." Ruth tried to spit out the proper sentiment. But Florence, as always, interrupted.

"Out with it, girl! There are people waiting. Do you think you're the only one at the funeral? Good Lord, you look ghastly. What have you done to your dress?" She reached over and tugged at Ruth's stiff arm, but Ruth held firm.

"I tore my dress," she whispered, hoping against hope that Florence would leave her alone.

"My word! How could you possibly tear your dress at a funeral, girl?" she shrilled. "What were you doing? Dancing?" Ruth's burning embarrassment flared into white-hot shame. She hung her head as tears of rage and helplessness scorched her eyes.

Florence smiled. It was a condescending smile, her interpretation of kindness.

"Well," she announced. "It's a hideous dress anyway. I wouldn't even give it to my house girls. But, as it was your mother's, no one can fault you for not being thrifty. And since you have no looks to speak of, at least you have that to your credit. Now run along, and do try not to look so miserable. It's bad enough to be burying Angus without having to put up with ill-looking mourners.

"By the way," she added as Ruth turned to go, "make sure you remind your father that I expect to see him at the meeting tomorrow, especially as he didn't have the courtesy to attend Angus's funeral. And tell him not to be late."

"Yes, Aunt Florence," whispered Ruth. How her aunt could possibly mention a business meeting at a time like this was beyond her.

"Please accept my condolences, Aunt Florence." She lowered her head and made for her buggy. She could feel the eyes of Annie's friends burning into her back. Florence turned triumphantly from Ruth and bore down on the girl standing closest to Annie.

"Why, Mary, how good of you to come."

Ruth hurried over to Chui, her horse, and unhitched him; then she turned to climb up into her buggy. Her head felt light and she was still unsteady on her feet. She stumbled and landed in the dust.

"Here, let me help you up, miss. You seem to be having a rather difficult day." Ruth scrambled awkwardly to her feet just as someone took her by the elbow. "Are you all right? You look really ill."

It was the tall stranger again. She turned and looked up into his face. Again, it was his eyes that drew her attention. He looked kindly down at, or rather right through, Ruth. She had the distinct impression she was being diagnosed.

"Are you feeling faint, miss? Perhaps you should lie down in the shade for a few minutes before you get on your way." He spoke with an American accent, one disconnected part of her mind noticed.

"Oh no, thank you," she sputtered, wiping dust out of her eyes. "I am just a little overcome by the funeral. He was my uncle. I'll be fine once I'm on my way." Ruth turned quickly to climb back up into the cart. She stopped. She couldn't do it without exposing her gaping tear. She turned and faced him.

"I've torn my dress," she explained helplessly.

To her surprise, he reached forward, picked her up by the waist, and placed her on the seat.

"Thank you," she said.

He lifted his hat. "Don't mention it. It's always my pleasure to help a lady in distress. Do you have far to go now?"

"Oh, no," she lied, and flicked her reins. The stranger tipped his hat again, but Ruth was too overcome to look at him. She just wanted to get away and be alone again as quickly as she could.

As she drove across the dry plain toward the blue hills shimmering tantalizingly in the distant heat, she relived over and over the humiliating encounter with Aunt Florence. Hot flushes of shame repeatedly washed over her skin, and now and then searing, angry tears scorched her cheeks. Automatically she scanned the sky, looking for rain clouds. Perhaps they might relieve some of her pain, washing it away with a storm and a flood of raging water. But it was too early for the rains, and there wasn't even the faintest scent of rain in the air. She drove past the baobab tree, squatting like an ugly blot on the otherwise lovely landscape. Even the guinea fowl scuttling out of her way only irritated her this afternoon.

The sun was dropping low over the hills on the other side of the plains behind her as she reached the bottom of the hillside. She was worn out with the memory of the afternoon and finally too tired to think through the pain again.

Her thoughts shifted to her meeting with the American stranger. She wondered who he was. She remembered how his blue eyes sparkled warmly when he spoke to her, and she smiled into the cool, green forest. *Yes,* she thought, *if I were pretty like Annie, that is the kind of man I would set my cap for.* And then, without warning, her whole being filled with an ache, a powerful, longing, yearning ache, and she wished with all her heart she wasn't driving alone up into the hills. *If it were possible for a woman like me to fall in love, that would be the man I would fall in love with. And if I did fall in love,* she thought to herself, flicking the reins, *I would chase him and follow him and relentlessly pursue him until he succumbed and fell in love with me. I would do whatever it took to capture him, and he wouldn't have a hope of escape.*

The songs of the birds in the trees were heart-wrenchingly lovely, Ruth thought as she drove through the dappled golden evening sunlight. They were singing only for her. The very air in the forest overflowed with their bittersweet melodies. She drove by the little path that led down the hill to the pool where she had seen the elephants yesterday. Remembering their joy, her heart filled once more with longing and she wondered if they would return. But it was getting dark, and she must hurry home. She hadn't eaten all day, and she knew that Milka would have supper ready. Her father would be angry if he were kept waiting.

three

Ruth saw her father off to town early the next morning with the milk wagon. He was dressed uncomfortably in a suit and tie, bought many years earlier when he was younger and leaner. His raw, freshly shaved face stuck out the top of his shirt. *He looks like a plucked, gooseflesh chicken, trussed and dressed, ready to roast,* Ruth noted, *and about as cheerful.*

"What do you think Florence wants?" she had asked him while they sat silently eating their steaming bowls of oatmeal under the watchful glare of the lion and the antelope.

"Humph," he grunted, shrugging his shoulders without looking up as he gulped down the dregs of his porridge. It seemed to Ruth that he had grown a crust or a shell around him. He had become hard and lifeless, someone that no longer had the capacity to communicate or love, just like one of his trophies on his wall.

Ruth stared at him, and the thought crossed her mind that perhaps there was only one thing that made him different from his trophies—the hopeless tragedy of his condition. After all, he was human, not an animal, a man who had been loved by his wife, her mother. A familiar wave of heart-sinking horror rose into her throat, and Ruth pushed away the thought that she was looking at herself thirty years on.

"It's clinic day," she'd announced suddenly, pushing her chair loudly away from her untouched porridge. Jack stood up, too, and strode out of the door. A weight of loneliness settled on Ruth's shoulders. Another day of hot, dry, hard work lay ahead. Mechanically Ruth set out to do it—but first there was her clinic to take care of.

She went out through the kitchen door to make sure Milka had all the household jobs under control, though it was more just to see a friendly, welcoming face. It had been years since Milka had questions about how to run the household.

Already there was a cluster of women and children from the compound waiting in the yard behind the house and in need of medical help. Despite their ailments, the women cheerfully chattered, and the children squealed as they chased loose chickens and a couple of the farm dogs.

Ruth always looked forward to days when she held her clinic. For many years, as she was growing up, she had dreamed of becoming a nurse; but as it was, there had never really been any choice. Her father always needed her; and anyway, there would never have been enough money to send her off to school. She still looked back to her dream now and then, but it was just a fleeting fantasy now, sweet and impossible. She had her clinic, and she was rewarded by the trust and gratitude of all the people on the farm. Memsahib Daktari they called her and sent their friends from the countryside all around to her clinic. Ruth managed to eke a little bit of pride out of that fact.

Today, however, as she surveyed the sea of turned-up faces in the front and the pleading eyes of mothers holding their babies in the background, she sensed that there was a little flurry of unusual interest somewhere in the crowd. Sure enough, a toto rushed up to Ruth with an envelope in his hand.

"*Memsahib Daktari,* for you alone." He spoke with the utmost solemnity and handed her the envelope. His dark brown eyes, wide and serious with the importance of his task, looked up at her. Ruth felt she should make a little bow in accepting such an important missive.

She opened the note and read.

Dear Ruthie,
    Would you join me for lunch at one o'clock? I
need to talk to you.

                                    Love, Annie

Ruth quickly scribbled an acceptance and returned it to the toto with a sixpence.

"For Memsahib Annie alone." She spoke in the same solemn tones and even returned his formal bow. The little boy scooted off in great glee with her note.

Ruth stood for a moment, thinking. She was puzzled about Annie. Annie was not in the habit of sending her notes or invitations to lunch. For a moment she wondered if there was any connection between this invitation and her father's errand in town this morning, but the totos were clamoring for her attention. Each one wanted to be the first to be treated by her. They pulled on her trousers and held up various parts of their bodies, wounded or swollen, and she was forced to pay attention to her task at hand.

After she had finished the clinic and given orders for the day's work, she went to her room to wash up. She stood stripped down to her underclothes in front of the closet. There were only two things hanging in there, her black funeral dress and a tweed skirt that her mother had brought with her as a young woman from Scotland. She had never dared to ask her father for money for anything else to wear because she knew exactly what his response would be. Her mother's clothes were good enough for her mother and should be good enough for her as well. End of discussion. Besides, Ruth went out in public so rarely that she had forced herself not to give the issue any thought. As she stood staring at the ugly, brown, scratchy, shapeless old skirt, she thought of how Annie would be dressed. She would probably wear a light cotton print that would make her look cool and as fresh as a dawn-lit forest, even in the middle of a dry spell like this. Ruth detested her old skirt with all her heart. The humiliation she had endured from Aunt Florence yesterday flared back into her mind, and she didn't think she could ever bear to go to town in her mother's old clothes again.

She reached for the skirt anyway. As she felt the warm tweed scratching against her fingers, a small seed of rebellion sprouted from the bed of bitterness in the bottom of her heart. She walked over to her dresser drawer, opened it, and pulled out a tiny pair of sewing scissors. Sitting deliberately on her bed, she took the scissors to the skirt, snapping and clipping at it with tiny, deadly snips. She cut right up the front from the hem to the waist, then she ripped off the waistband. She took the rest of the skirt and snipped and ripped until there was nothing left of it but little triangles and squares of tweed scattered on the bed and the floor all around her.

Well, she thought, surveying her work, that feels fine. She strode over to the chest of drawers and pulled out a pair of clean khaki trousers and a crisp white shirt.

When she was dressed, she picked up her hat to leave the room. If she had had a mirror in her room, she would have seen a surprisingly fresh and attractive young woman. But guilt for what she had done to her mother's skirt was already beginning to settle like cold, gray silt in her mind. She swept up the remains of the dress and stuffed them in the back of her bottom drawer. She had wantonly destroyed a piece of her mother's sacred memory. Shame swirled through her mind and heart. She pulled her old hat low over her eyes and slunk outside to saddle her horse.

It was a long, hot, midday ride down the valley to town. She hoped she wouldn't see her father on his way back home, and she was relieved when she reached the driveway of the Campbell estate, just before the outskirts of town. She turned into a wide, tree-lined boulevard and into the soft, cool shade that rained down onto her like the tiny purple petals falling from the flowers when the breeze whispered through the jacaranda trees above. Ruth breathed the scented air greedily.

She could see the red tile roof of the house on the hill at the end of the driveway. The jacarandas led up to lush gardens with spacious, green lawns and huge, shady trees placed strategically here and there. The house itself stood in a pool of color. Blooms and buds of every sort of flower rippled in the wind. Off in the distance, the shining river wound past the town of Campbellburgh.

Ruth pulled the buggy up at the veranda steps and got down awkwardly. She stood for a moment, looking at the elegant furniture on the veranda, regretting what she had done to her tweed skirt. *How could I have come to lunch in trousers?* she thought, as a red-hot rush of embarrassment flooded her cheeks. *Perhaps I could turn around and go home. I could send some excuse with a toto.* But just then, the door flew open and Annie rushed out to greet her.

"Ruthie! Thank you so much for coming!" As Ruth had predicted, Annie was a vision of loveliness. Her long, golden mane was swept softly back into a large roll behind, and she wore a beautiful, pale blue dress with soft, flowing sleeves and a wide skirt that rustled crisply as she walked, or rather ran. She threw her arms around Ruth and gave her a welcoming hug.

"Ruthie! I'm so glad you could come. It's been ages and ages since we've had a chance for a chat. How are you? You look wonderful!" She surveyed Ruth from head to toe. "I wish I could bring off wearing trousers the way you do. You're so lucky to be tall and slim!" Ruth smiled. *I should have known.* Annie could always make her feel better.

"Come in, have some squash, and cool off. Lunch is almost ready. You're probably starving." Annie took Ruth by the arm and led her inside. The cool air of the house rushed out the open door to meet them. Ruth adjusted her eyes to the dark room. Silk-covered settees were scattered tastefully here and there, more to be admired than sat upon, Ruth thought. There were little round tables of dark wood polished so thoroughly that they perfectly reflected the elegant china figurines or bouquets of flowers that sat daintily upon them. Annie negotiated her way around the furniture and led Ruth through the French doors at the far end of the room and out onto the patio.

Two places were set out for lunch, with yet another vase of flowers on a wicker and glass table under a large, fragrant frangipani tree. Annie and Ruth sat on wicker chairs with pretty chintz cushions. The lawn spread out before them as smooth as a lake on a calm day, right down to a little arbor covered with flowery vines, a rather inadequate foil against the powerfully green, lush jungle behind. Ruth couldn't see the river, but the jungle was watered by it as it wound its way around to Campbellburgh. Every time the air stirred, she caught the damp, heavy river scent rolling up the lawn toward them.

Annie was already chattering away a mile a minute. She asked Ruth all the usual questions about her father and the farm and the weather this year, but Ruth noticed a hollowness to her voice. Annie paused only long enough to register Ruth's answer before quickly flitting onto the next question. Ruth sipped on her orange squash and wondered what was the matter with Annie.

She was relieved when lunch was served and Annie paused long enough to let Ruth help herself to the cold cuts and jellied salads that were being brought in one after the other. Ruth piled her plate high. Each dish seemed so fresh and enticing after Milka's heavy Scottish cooking, which was more suited to cold, dark winters than tropical afternoons. Each time a new platter was offered, Ruth felt she just couldn't resist. Annie looked on smiling and helped herself to some fruit and cheese. When the platters finally stopped coming, Ruth looked down at her plate and blushed, but Annie put her hand across the table onto Ruth's arm.

"Ruth, you work out on the farm all day long; you have to eat properly to keep up your strength, and you don't have an ounce of fat on you. And look at me. I eat like a bird, do nothing all day, and the mere sight of food adds inches onto my waistline."

Ruth looked wryly down at her plate. "Well, don't look in this direction, then." Annie laughed her old bubbly contagious laugh, and Ruth realized it was the first time she had heard Annie laugh since she arrived. She was ashamed that she hadn't even asked her how things were now with her father gone.

"Annie, how are you? It must be an awfully difficult time for you." Ruth spoke seriously and Annie stopped laughing. A shadow passed across her face.

Annie's voice was suddenly low and unhappy, "I think I am all right, Ruthie, but I'm quite worried about Mother. She is not herself at all; but I suppose with all she's been through, it's very understandable. All the same, you know how difficult she can be?"

Ruth nodded, restraining herself from commenting on Florence's behavior. Annie went on.

"She has become very strange the last few days, and I am frankly worried about her sanity. That is what I wanted to talk to you about." Annie leaned forward. "Do you know that I am not allowed to leave the house?" she whispered.

Ruth let her fork clatter down onto her plate. "What do you mean, Annie?" *Annie must be exaggerating* was the first thought that came to Ruth's mind. Aunt Florence couldn't be that bad, not to Annie, who was always given anything she ever wanted or needed. But Annie continued.

"You know Jimmy MacRae, don't you? He and I have been friends for a long time. We got to know each other at church, mostly. Jimmy takes his Christian faith very seriously, and I have come to admire him a great deal because of it. We spend a lot of time together discussing the meaning of life and what it means to love and serve God. We began to discover that we had a lot in common. Ruthie, I wish you could know him as I do. He is such a fine Christian and such a wonderful person." Ruth smiled. Was there anybody about whom Annie had anything bad to say?

"Anyway," Annie went on, "a few weeks ago he asked me to marry him. I was so surprised, Ruthie! I didn't know what to say. I had never thought of him in that way before. But as I got over my surprise, I began to realize that I really was in love with him, and I couldn't possibly ask for a finer Christian man to be my husband. Oh, I was so happy!"

Ruth was astonished to hear how sad Annie's voice was as she spoke the last words.

Annie paused and composed herself before she went on. "I accepted Jimmy's proposal, and he came to ask Father for my hand. Father gave him permission. He always had a secret soft spot for Jimmy, and he would never have denied me anything to make me happy. But when Mother was told what Father had done, she was livid. She has never had even the time of day for the MacRaes, what with their bad luck and never being quite well-off enough to suit her.

"It was the day after that when Father took his turn for the worse. Mother insisted that it was the effect of Jimmy's visit on him. And now that Father has died, she is blaming Jimmy and me for it. She actually says that Jimmy only wants to marry me for the money he thinks I will inherit!"

Annie pulled out a lace handkerchief and buried her face in it. Ruth looked away. She felt desperately sorry for Annie, but she didn't know what to do when Annie started to cry. What could she do to make Annie feel better? Her thoughts rushed around in a panic. She didn't know where to look when people cried, no matter how much she cared, and Annie's problem was so far out of her depth! But she must do something. Annie was sobbing, and with each breath she took, Ruth felt her own heart slowly breaking painfully open. She took a deep breath; she couldn't stand it any longer.

"Annie, Annie, don't cry." Ruth reached forward awkwardly and put her hand on Annie's arm. Why, oh why, hadn't Annie chosen to unburden herself on someone more helpful?

"Oh, Ruthie!" Annie looked up out of her handkerchief into Ruth's panic-stricken face. "Mother has forbidden me to see Jimmy or even leave the house. And she won't let me see my friends from church alone because she says she doesn't trust them. Ruthie, I am afraid the strain of losing Father has made my mother a little mad! I can't understand why she is behaving like this.

"And the worst of it is that Jimmy came over to see Mother the day after Father passed away. He wanted to see if he could do anything to help her or to make things better." To Ruth's horror, Annie put her face back into her handkerchief and sobbed as if her heart had broken all over again. Ruth could only sit and watch her, paralyzed with embarrassment and pity. But, suddenly to her immense relief, Annie took a deep shuddering breath and stopped sobbing.

"Mother was awful to him! She shouted at him to leave and accused him to his face of marrying me for my money and of killing my father. But Jimmy was wonderful in the face of it all. He explained to Mother that he only ever wanted to make me happy and that we loved each other and that if I had changed my mind since my Father's death, he would never again bring up the subject of our marriage.

"Mother told him that he had better never bring it up again if he knew what was good for him. And she ordered Juma to throw Jimmy out of the house. And that is when I came in. I had been standing outside the door listening. I couldn't help it. I came in and told Mother that I loved Jimmy and he loved me and that I intended to marry him no matter what she said. I have never stood up to Mother like that before.

"Oh, Ruthie, I was just as shocked as she was! She just stood there with her mouth open. But before my very eyes, she gathered herself together and she turned cold. I don't know how else to describe it, but I saw it happen. She turned to ice, and I was afraid, Ruthie.

"That was when I wavered. I just became afraid of her and I wanted to stop her from being so cold and cruel—I just wanted it to end! I told her I didn't want to disobey her, and I would never want to hurt her, and I really didn't want to lose my family by marrying Jimmy. But she didn't let me finish. She turned to Jimmy and ordered him to leave the house. Jimmy looked at me before he went, and I wanted to tell him I loved him, but I was paralyzed. She had turned me to ice, too." Tears were running down Annie's cheeks again.

"I just stood there, and Jimmy looked at me and he said, 'I love you, Annie,' and he left. And I just stood there like a stone watching him go." Annie stopped and regained her control over the tears. Ruth waited for her in silence.

"Then Mother turned to me and said that until I renounced him, I would not leave the house except to go to the funeral. That was three days ago, and since then, it has been a nightmare, Ruthie. I have told her again and again that I won't disobey her and marry Jimmy without her consent, but she refuses to believe a word I say! She is sure I am plotting against her." Annie put her face into her hands and cried, "I just had to tell someone, Ruthie. I don't understand what has happened to her."

Ruth wanted to get up and put her arms around Annie and hug her, but she couldn't make herself move. She tried to speak.

"Annie," she began, but she had to clear her throat. "Annie," she tried again, "have you written to Jimmy and told him how things are?"

Annie burst into a renewed outbreak of sobs, and Ruth waited, mute with embarrassment at seeing the effect of her question on her cousin.

"She's instructed all the servants that I am not to be allowed to get or to send any letters, and I know Jimmy has sent me something because I saw her receive a letter from the houseboy at the MacRae place. She tore it up." Annie paused; then in a low, calm voice, she went on, "Ruthie, I think Mother has actually gone mad. She is holding me a prisoner in my own home, and she won't believe me or trust me. I am frightened, Ruthie. I am frightened for her even more than I am for myself. She seems to have crossed over into some mad sort of place since Father has gone, and no one knows it but me.

"That's why I wanted to tell you, Ruthie. You are family. I couldn't let anyone else in town know what is happening. It is too shameful. She is too proud for that kind of information to ever get about. Really, I don't want to hurt her." Annie sat back in her chair. She suddenly looked exhausted, but she was no longer crying.

Ruth felt as though she were reeling backward. How could she possibly help Annie? What could she say?

"Perhaps if you just give her a little time, she will get over it," Ruth ventured timidly.

"I had thought at first that would help," replied Annie tiredly, "but somehow I have the feeling that there is more to it than that. She's getting worse, not better. As soon as Father died she became so strange. Dr. Mowatt came over, but he wasn't terribly sober, you know what he is, and he really wasn't much help at all. He just gave her some more sleeping pills and told me that 'Time heals all.'

"And then there is this odd business with Douglas MacPherson. She seems to have taken a very strange dislike to the poor man. I know him quite well because he comes to church. He is a friend of Jimmy's and mine. Anyway, just because he doesn't want to marry the first woman he meets in Campbellburgh is no reason to dislike him with such passion. Besides, he is a confirmed bachelor. He doesn't want to marry anyone. A man has a right to live as he chooses.

"But Dr. MacPherson is wealthy, and Mother started scheming from the first moment she laid eyes on him. When he refused to go along with her plans, she flew into a temper. She vowed to run him out of town before she would allow him to build that hospital of his. I shudder to think what she is up to at that meeting today."

Ruth was puzzled. "Who is Douglas MacPherson?" She had never heard his name before.

Annie looked at her in surprise. "My goodness, Ruthie, you really are too isolated up there on that farm of yours! Douglas came to town a month ago! He is a Canadian missionary doctor and very rich. Mother tried her best to marry me off to him; but as I said, I don't think he intends to marry anyone. All he wants to do is buy the land down by the river, next to the railway station. When Mother and Father discovered what he intended to do with it, they absolutely refused to sell the land to him."

"What does he want to do with it?" asked Ruth, still confused.

"He wants to build a hospital for the African people since they suffer so terribly with European diseases and yet have almost no access to proper medicine. It is a noble and Christian enterprise, and I hope he succeeds in it! But

Mother says it will ruin the entire town to have a filthy hospital for Africans right in the center of it. They have cured their own diseases with witch doctors since creation and they should continue to do it that way. It would only confuse them to make them submit to modern medical practices. Besides, she says a hospital would attract them from all over the countryside. They'll clog up the railway and pollute the river. The tourist business will be completely ruined! No one will want to come and stay at Daddy's hotel or arrange safaris from Campbellburgh, and we will become destitute! Everything that the family has worked so long and hard for will go right down the drain.

"And don't for a minute doubt that Mother can't stop him. After all, we Campbells do have first refusal rights on all the land inside the town limits, and I can't imagine any of the farmers outside town daring to stand up against Mother. After all, can you imagine how difficult she would make it for them to do any business in town?"

"So that's what she called the meeting in town for today, then." Ruth spoke more to herself. "She probably wanted my father there because of Mother's land." As an original Campbell, her mother had been given a lot within the town limits. It was an undeveloped piece on the river next to the church. Upon her mother's death, her father had, of course, inherited it, even though he was not actually a Campbell by blood. No doubt he was still bound by the Campbell rights for first refusal.

Annie was now surprised. "Your father owns land in Campbellburgh?"

Just then there was a loud clattering of wheels, and they heard Florence shouting orders at her servants.

"Good gracious, look at the time!" Annie jumped up, panic stricken. "We've been chatting far too long. Mother will have my hide! I am forbidden to have visitors."

Ruth stood up as well. "Don't worry, Annie," she said, sounding braver than she felt. "I'll just tell her that I was passing through and I dropped in for lunch. It's only me. I'm not really a visitor, as you said before, I'm just family." But the thought of a confrontation with her aunt, especially after what Annie had just told her about her state of mind, sent a chill of fear into the pit of Ruth's stomach. She silently stood next to Annie as the two of them listened to Florence sweep into the drawing room. A moment later the doors to the patio flew open.

Turning immediately on Ruth, she swept her eyes from the top of her short, unruly, red hair, down past her white shirt and khaki trousers, to her dusty old boots, and snorted with disdain.

"What, may I ask, are you doing here? Annie is to receive no visitors!" She spoke as though Ruth were deliberately disobeying her.

"I was just passing by on my way home," stammered Ruth.

"Well, I suppose as it is only you, I'll make an exception. Only see to it that you don't come back. If you intend to meddle in Annie's affairs, let me warn you, young lady, you'll pay for it!"

"I must go now, Aunt Florence," said Ruth quickly. She flashed a helpless smile at Annie. "Thank you for inviting me for lunch."

Annie smiled back weakly, but Florence boomed at Ruth, "You were in town today? I never saw you arrive with your father. I trust you are not conniving behind his back. It is impossible to trust any young people these days, not even one's own children." She glared significantly at Annie, her face as hard and rigid as a mask.

Ruth wanted to get as far away as quickly as she could. "Good-bye," she whispered and slunk past her aunt like a dog with its tail between its legs. As she scuttled through the drawing room, she could hear Florence. Her voice was different. Annie was right. It was colder than ice. A splinter off her voice sliced right through the cool air of the drawing room and struck Ruth between the shoulder blades as she ran to the door. She felt suddenly wounded and sick. She hurried Chui at a trot down the soft lane of jacarandas.

She trotted briskly over the grassy plains. When she at last came to the bottom of the hill and the road wound alongside the river again, Ruth allowed herself to think over what Annie had told her. She found she could hardly contain her anger at Aunt Florence for treating Annie so shamefully. *If only I were stronger and more courageous.* Ruth bit her lip and kicked Chui to hurry up. She was angry and frustrated at her own helplessness. And Annie's. *Silly, trusting Annie. She should have chosen a better person to confide her plight to—someone who actually had the courage and the power to do something about it. What could I do to help her? Absolutely and completely nothing. Nothing at all.*

The air was scented and cooler up here on the hillside in the shade of the trees, and Chui, knowing that they were getting close to home, walked a little faster. The wide, slow river had shrunk into Ruth's own stream again, and it bubbled cheerily beside the road and over the smooth, slippery stones. Slowly, Ruth began to realize there might be something she could do for Annie. She could at least go and see Jimmy MacRae and explain to him what Annie had told her. Perhaps between the two of them they could come up with a way to help Annie, even a little bit. *Yes,* she decided, as Chui emerged from the forest and the farmhouse came into view, *I will go over to the MacRae place and see Jimmy tomorrow.*

four

Ruth was mildly surprised that evening when her father wasn't home in time for supper. Rather than eating in the dining room alone under the glowering glares of the animal heads, she took her supper in the steamy, noisy kitchen with Milka and her toto. The plain boiled meat and vegetables seemed dull and bland compared with lunch at the Campbells', but Ruth relived every dish and each mouthful of lunch for Milka's benefit. She told Milka of Annie's predicament and Florence's invitation to Douglas MacPherson. Milka rolled her eyes in disgust.

"Jimmy MacRae is a fine Christian. Memsahib Campbell should be glad that her daughter wants to marry a man like that. It doesn't matter what his father was like, he will do well, I know. He is a very hard worker. I have a cousin who works for young Bwana MacRae, and he admires him very much.

"But Memsahib Campbell never learned to look at anyone else but herself. She will make very many mistakes that way, especially now that her *bwana* is gone." Milka stood up and took away Ruth's empty plate.

"Bwana said he would be home for supper. I wonder what he is doing."

"It is strange," Ruth replied with a small twinge of uneasiness. "Perhaps he stopped at the hotel for a drink. He may have lost track of the time." Ruth noticed lately that her father's drinking had begun to control his life, and his word had become rather unreliable.

"Yes, I am afraid that is what has happened." Milka

looked pityingly at Ruth, but Ruth stood up to go.

"I am going to town tomorrow," she said. "I am going to see Bwana Jimmy about Annie."

Milka clucked her lips and shook her head with disapproval. "You know Memsahib Campbell," she said ominously. "She finds out everything sooner or later. And when she learns you have been speaking to Bwana MacRae about Miss Annie, she will be very angry and she will make your life a miserable thing. She is almost as bad as a witch doctor, even worse perhaps. You watch out, *'Sabu!* I will have to stay up all night in prayer if you are not careful!"

"Florence Campbell couldn't really do too much to make my life more miserable than it is already, so don't you worry about me, Milka," Ruth laughed. Suddenly it felt surprisingly pleasant to be risking the ire of Florence Campbell in order to help Annie. She marched boldly out of the kitchen and tossed a look of scorn at the glare of the lion in the dining room.

The door burst open and Kamau rushed in. "*Bwana's* been hurt! Come quickly, *'Sabu!*"

Ruth crashed back to reality and rushed after Kamau into the lounge, where her father was stumbling toward the couch. He must be very drunk, she judged by the way he staggered and the stream of foul language coming from his mouth. His face was covered in mud and blood. He'd gotten drunk and fallen off his horse.

With more disgust than pity, Ruth hurried over and helped him to the couch. It was then that she saw his leg. His torn trouser leg was soaked in blood, and he was dragging it on the ground like a lifeless thing.

"What on earth happened to you, Father? How did you get hurt?" She turned to Kamau. "Quickly get hot water, clean cloths, and bring me the dawa from the cupboard."

Jack groaned as he lay on the couch, and Ruth realized he

was in great pain. His skin, what she could see of it, was unnaturally white. A stab of fear tore through her heart. Jack most reluctantly submitted to Ruth's ministrations, cursing and spluttering every time she touched the cuts on his face. They turned out to be fairly superficial. It was the mud that made it all look worse.

"What about your leg, Father?" she asked. "What happened?" He was losing blood fast, and the couch was already soaked and red.

"Leave my leg alone." Jack emitted a vicious growl. "And pass me a whiskey!" Ruth fetched him a glass of whiskey to relieve some of his pain. She carefully cut the leg off his trousers. Not only was his thigh torn open, but she guessed that the bone was broken badly and would need to be set.

"Cursed motorcars," he began, speaking, or rather growling, more to himself than to Ruth. She listened. "They should be run off the road. I was just riding along, minding my own business, down by the Campbells' place, when I hear this great roaring noise behind me. It didn't sound like any animal I'd ever heard, so I assumed it was one of those automobile contraptions. It was a long way off, or so I thought, when suddenly around the bend, right behind me, here it comes, like he owned the road! Simba reared and I came off, more from shock than anything else."

Ruth thought uncharitably that if he hadn't been drunk, he would have kept his mount.

"I certainly couldn't blame Simba," he was saying. "It was that maniac driving that motorcar." Jack paused to take a couple more swigs from his glass and compose himself.

"Oh, my leg hurts! Don't you dare touch it!" He snapped at Ruth as she stood up to look at it again. She stopped in her tracks.

"I had better send for Dr. Mowatt, Father. I am pretty sure it is broken."

"What! That old coot? I might as well just lay myself down and die, for all he can do for me. He kills more people than he saves. Look how much he did for old Angus Campbell!" Jack snorted with derision.

"But, Father, no one could have saved Uncle Angus, and Dr. Mowatt did all he could." Ruth tried to speak in her most reasonable tone of voice, but it had the opposite effect from what she had intended.

"So, you're trying to kill me, are you? You can't wait to see your inheritance, is that it? Or maybe you just want to be rid of your old man? After all, I'm just a chain around your neck these days, don't think I can't tell. Perhaps you're right. It would save a fortune in doctor fees if I died now, wouldn't it? Ask Florence Campbell, if you don't believe me!"

"Father!" Ruth was horrified. "How could you say such things? I only wanted to have your leg looked at because it is broken. I didn't know what else to suggest."

She watched silently as her father finished his drink; and without being asked, she got up and refilled his glass. He took it absentmindedly and continued with the story of his accident as if the subject had never changed.

"Simba bolted, right over me and back down the road, and the car came to a stop just inches, inches from my head! A fine sight, I tell you.

"Well, lo and behold." Jack's voice prickled up with sarcasm like the spikes on a hedgehog. "Who should step out of it but our Dr. Douglas MacPherson, all dressed up to the nines like he was going to meet the queen. He was all apologies and 'may I help you, sirs,' but I wouldn't have any of it. Not from him, after what he's been up to, and then throwing me off my horse like that."

Ruth snapped to attention. "What's he been up to, Father?" she asked quietly.

"He's trying to buy up the entire town and turn it into

some sort of haven for blacks. He's probably connected with some secret organization to try to incite the natives into rebellion against the British. Building hospitals and schools and what have you, so he says. Campbellburgh is right at the center of everything with the railway and the river. Why, if he got our blacks armed and going, we could have a full-scale rebellion on our hands before we knew where we were. We'd all be murdered in our beds!"

Jack held out his glass for more whiskey, and Ruth got up to fetch it for him. "Who on earth told you this, Father?" She handed him another full glass.

"It's all over town; everyone knows. That's why Florence called the meeting today. She's going to stop him. And a good thing, too. He'll have a fight on his fancy American hands if he tries to take us on." Jack chuckled happily. He was beginning to feel no pain. It was the drink.

"The man is a monster, and both he and that monstrous car should be run out of town. I'd be the one to do it, too, but for what he's done to my leg. I think Simba stepped on it. But I don't blame her. It was that motorcar that frightened her."

"Father, you must let me look at it again," Ruth pleaded. "If Simba stepped on it, it is certainly broken. We must fetch Dr. Mowatt." Jack knocked back the last half of his glass and lay back on the couch. Ruth took it as a sign that he was ready to be examined.

Jack was drenched with blood. His entire thigh was swollen, and the gash ran down almost the whole length of it and was full of dirt.

"Father, we must get you to the hospital at once. You will have an infection in that gash by morning. You need some stitching, and the bone must be set by a doctor."

"Hah, you'll never get me to that hospital. If it's my time to go, I'll go alone. Just get me another drink, will you?" Ruth ignored him.

"Well, we at least need to get Dr. Mowatt," she pleaded. "This is extremely serious. Your leg will be infected soon. I don't know how you even managed to ride home. How did you catch Simba?" Ruth stood amazed at the strength of character that could make a man ride so far in such pain. Reconsidering, she handed him another drink. Maybe, she rationalized, it would not only keep the pain down, but it might fight infection that would surely set in quickly. She would send Kamau for Dr. Mowatt at first light, no matter what her father said.

"MacPherson caught him for me. A fine sight he was, too, all covered with sweat and dust. I don't know where he was off to all dressed up like that, but he won't be making much of an impression when he gets there." Jack chuckled wickedly to himself at the memory.

"He tried to make me go with him. Said he was a doctor and he could make sure I was all right, but he was probably waiting for the chance to do me in completely, having failed the first time."

Ruth washed and patched the wound as well as she could. He must have lost a lot of blood. She settled him on the couch for the night. The whiskey had done the trick, and within a very short time, he was sleeping fitfully.

❧

Before dawn Ruth woke with a sense of foreboding, which had settled into the pit of her stomach through the night. It weighed her down like a stone as she heaved herself wearily out of bed. She had been awake often through the night and had checked her father several times. He had been sleeping very fitfully.

She made her way down the hall in the gray morning light. The grayness made everything look ugly and grim. She slipped quietly into the lounge and stood motionless behind the sofa. She had the horrible fear that her father would be lying dead. After a few minutes, she could see the blanket rising and falling steadily and rhythmically. Letting out a long breath of relief, she tiptoed back to her bedroom. She was surprised at herself for being so nerve-racked. *I'm turning into a fussy old spinster,* she thought, irritated.

Kamau was already waiting faithfully for her in the kitchen when she arrived a little while later. She sent him off to town to fetch Dr. Mowatt as quickly as he could. The sense of foreboding in the pit of her stomach turned into a fear-burdened loneliness in the silent, empty kitchen. She sat down heavily at the kitchen table and waited for Milka to arrive.

Suddenly the loneliness rose in her throat, and tears filled her eyes. She put her head down on the table and sobbed. She couldn't bear it if anything should happen to her father. She would be all alone. It's true, he wasn't much company these days; but the thought of living up here on the farm alone, day in and day out, year in and year out, was frightening beyond belief. She stared with horror down the road stretching out before her straight and narrow, arid and endless.

There was a scuffling of feet in the hall, then the kitchen door burst open and in bustled Milka. Ruth jumped with surprise. "Milka, you startled me!"

"Lord have mercy! *'Sabu* Ruth!" Milka exclaimed in surprise. "What are you doing here frightening the living daylights out of me like that?" But when she saw the look on Ruth's face, she instantly became worried. "Your father, is he all right?"

"He's still sleeping. I don't know, but I'm worried about that gash on his leg. It's pretty deep, I'm afraid. And the bone is broken. I hope Dr. Mowatt gets here soon. I told Kamau to make him hurry."

Milka came over to Ruth and put her arm around her

shoulders. "Don't worry, 'Sabu Ruth. Everything will turn out just fine, you'll see. I have been praying for you."

"Ah, Milka." Ruth smiled up into the kind, loving eyes of her friend. "If I thought God cared about me as much as you do, I wouldn't worry. But even you don't have the power of God over life and death."

Milka laughed. "I wouldn't be so sure that God doesn't love you, 'Sabu Ruth. You'd be surprised what He will do for us when we ask. Just you watch." Milka's laugh, loud and sure, filled the whole kitchen, and the heaviness that had been gripping Ruth all morning loosed its hold a little. She straightened her shoulders and sat at her usual place at the table. Life had regained some perspective with Milka's words. Even if she didn't believe in God, she believed in Milka's loving-kindness.

It was only halfway through the morning when Ruth heard the sound of a motorcar in the distance. Her father hadn't been awake very long, and Ruth was trying to get him to eat some of Milka's porridge. He was in considerable pain. His leg looked worse and was very swollen. Ruth knew she would somehow have to persuade him not only to let the doctor see it, but also to go to the hospital in Nairobi.

The motorcar was almost there. Dr. Mowatt traveled by buggy, and she wondered who would be coming up to the farm in a car. Perhaps Dr. Mowatt had understood the urgency of the situation and persuaded this Douglas MacPherson to bring him here, she thought as she ran outside onto the veranda. She could hear the wheels churning up the soft dirt on the cart track. A plume of reddish-brown dust billowed up from below the brow of the hill.

Slowly, a sleek, black car appeared in the distance, and Ruth watched fascinated as it drove up to the front of the house with Kamau sitting proudly in the front seat next to the driver. Where was Dr. Mowatt? Surely Kamau hadn't returned without Dr. Mowatt? The car pulled up to a halt in front of the steps, and Kamau jumped out.

"Jambo, Memsahib!" he called excitedly, but Ruth was furious.

"Kamau, where is Dr. Mowatt? Why didn't you come back with Dr. Mowatt?"

"Excuse me, ma'am." It was the driver. Ruth glared at him as he walked around the car toward them. She was angry to be interrupted at such a desperate moment. He put out his hand to shake hers. "Dr. Mowatt is delivering a baby on one of the outlying farms. You'll just have to make do with me, I'm afraid. I'm Dr. Douglas MacPherson." Ruth didn't move.

"I believe we've met before, but I didn't have the pleasure of learning your name." Ruth stood stupefied, recognizing the stranger who had helped her onto the buggy at Angus Campbell's funeral. Surely there was a mistake. This couldn't be Dr. MacPherson. But he was standing there in front of her holding out his hand.

"Ruth," she replied quietly. "Are you really a doctor?" she asked.

"As I live and breathe" came the quick reply. "Now lead me to the patient. I understand there is some urgency."

"Yes, come with me," said Ruth, turning back into the house. This was not what she was expecting. She'd never known any other doctor but Dr. Mowatt. She had no idea what her father would do when he laid eyes on Douglas MacPherson again, but she really had no choice.

"I am terribly sorry about your father," he said, following her inside. "The whole thing was entirely my fault, and I am sick at the pain I have caused you and your father." Ruth stood in front of the couch where her father lay. She breathed a sigh of relief—he had fallen back asleep. While Dr. Mac-Pherson bent over to look at her father's leg, she forced herself to look at him. He was a big man with broad shoulders and a head of thick, sandy hair, blown straight backwards from the wind of the motorcar. But he had gentle hands and a genuinely kind face as he carefully looked over Jack.

"I had no idea he was hurt this badly!" He straightened up looking shocked. "How could he have possibly gotten back up to the farm with a broken leg? If he had only let me take a look at it, I would never have let him do it. I'm terribly sorry about it all. I took the corner too fast, not really expecting that there would be anyone out riding such a lonely road. Please accept my apologies, Miss Jones."

"It's not too badly broken, I hope," Ruth replied politely, without any conviction.

"I'm afraid your dad isn't in very good shape," he replied seriously.

My dad! Ruth had never dreamed of being so familiar with him. She always called him "Father." Dr. MacPherson bent over again and touched the wound ever so carefully. Jack woke up, and Ruth braced herself for the worst. It wasn't long in coming.

"What do you think you're doing here?" Jack's eyes flew open, and he spat the words out like venom. But, as he was unable to lift himself off the couch, they lost some of their potency. Dr. MacPherson ignored his greeting and calmly replied that Dr. Mowatt was busy and, since he was the only other doctor in town, he had come.

"Perhaps, in some small way I can make amends for what I did to you yesterday."

He may as well save his breath, Ruth thought to herself. *Father never listens to apologies.* But to Ruth's utter amazement, her father slowly laid back down, closed his eyes, and cursed quietly under his breath.

Not realizing the enormity of what had just occurred, Dr.

MacPherson continued examining her father's leg. Ruth stood staring. Either this Douglas MacPherson had cast some sort of a spell over him, or her father was much sicker than she had realized.

After a short while, Dr. MacPherson looked up at her. "Miss Jones, your dad is in serious need of medical care, much more than I am able to give him here. He will be okay, but we must take him to a hospital right away."

He was speaking to her quietly and firmly. "He's broken his thigh, and the gash is getting infected already. We had better get him to the hospital in Nairobi today. I'll take him in my car. Get some blankets and some water. We should leave at once."

Ruth looked at her father's face. It was so white that his freckles stood out individually like patches of mold on pale cheese. She had never seen him look so ill. In fact, until now, she would never have believed it was possible to bring him so low. He had always been in charge and, even in the depth of his drink, he still had a menacing sense of control. It was frightening to see him so helpless, and a fresh wave of fear surged up from the depths of Ruth's stomach. But they would get him to Nairobi. Dr. MacPherson would get him there and everything would be fine.

Dr. MacPherson looked up to see that she was still standing, staring at her father's leg.

"Miss Jones." He stood up slowly, and touched her on the shoulder. "Please don't worry. We'll take him to the hospital and they will fix him up just like new. Come along, now." He spoke to her slowly and compassionately, and she was enveloped with an overwhelming sense of gratitude to him for helping her father. She wanted to reach out and hug him and thank him for being so hopeful. Instead, she rushed off to fetch the blankets.

She quickly pulled blankets from the chest in her father's

bedroom. Her heart was flooded with strange feelings. Oh, how right she had been about Douglas MacPherson at Angus's funeral! She did like him! Thoughts swirled about her head. It must be the sleepless night that is making me feel so odd. Somehow, she had to control herself. *How can I be thinking this way when Father is so ill?*

She came back into the lounge with an armload of blankets. Dr. MacPherson and Kamau were already carrying her father to the backseat of the car. He looked so small and fragile in their arms. They eased him inside the back of the car, and Ruth covered him gently with a blanket. It was horrifying to see how quickly he could diminish into this poor, old, sick man. He just closed his eyes when she covered him. Not even a whine or a murmur passed his lips. *Please, Milka's God, help us to get him to the hospital safely,* Ruth prayed silently.

Dr. MacPherson was standing at the open front door of the car waiting for her. She slipped quickly inside. The leather seats crinkled softly as she stiffly settled back into their luxurious embrace. The pungent aroma of hot leather swirled about her. All the dials and meters gleamed importantly in the polished wooden dashboard before her. Dr. MacPherson got in beside her. He pushed down on one of the pedals on the floor, and the car purred and moved slowly forward. There was a moan from the backseat.

"Are you all right, Father?" asked Ruth, turning around to look at him.

A low, angry growl was the only reply, and Ruth sighed with relief and hope.

"We'll get him there as quickly as we can." Dr. MacPherson spoke soothingly to her, and she was ashamed of the sudden urge she felt to reach out and hold onto him. She looked down at her large, sunburned hands clutched nervously in her lap.

They were flying down the road faster than Ruth had ever been in her life. All the familiar turns and trees and bumps in the road were rushing swiftly past. A huge cloud of dust churned behind them, and the engine roared and whined as they negotiated the curves in the road. Ruth held tightly to a small handle on the door beside her.

It was a breathtaking ride. Ruth felt that she was in a world by herself, cut off from everyone and everything around her by a wall of noise and speed. At the bottom of the hillside, before they reached the Nairobi road turnoff, a stand of Masai stood at attention, watching them pass. Their red blankets and feathered headgear suddenly blew in the breeze of the passing car. Then as Ruth looked over her shoulder, they were swallowed by dust and disappeared from sight. A few guinea fowl scuttled into the dry bush beside the road. Ruth could hear their indignant squawks over the roar of the engine, but only for a moment as they, too, were lost to the dust behind them.

At last they slowed and turned onto the long, straight Nairobi road, and Ruth noticed that the countryside became bigger. A purple hill, with the typical cone shape of a volcano, appeared far away on the plain to the right. Off in the distance ahead of her loomed the blue-green ridge of the escarpment where they were headed. Their big black motorcar shrank in comparison to this vast landscape. It seemed to Ruth that they were only a tiny beetle inching its way slowly across the wide, dry plain, never noticeably getting closer to the wall of the escarpment or any farther past the volcano in the dusty distance.

The thorn trees on the plain slowly stalked past, holding up the sky with their tabletop branches. Now and then they passed a giraffe or two nibbling on the lower leaves. As the motorcar approached the giraffes, they loped away, their huge necks and legs moving in slow motion. They drove past herds of antelope, which bounded quickly out of sight and into the grasses. And still they flew on.

The rolling plain and the roar of the engine were having a calming effect on Ruth's nerves. She felt soothed and peaceful. She drifted farther and farther into her own world, still isolated by the sound and the speed. Nothing touched her. The warm sun shone down through the windshield, and the breeze blew into her face. She closed her eyes. Everything was going to be fine. *How different life looks in the heat of the day,* she thought to herself as she remembered the sense of fear and panic with which she had awakened in the cold, gray predawn.

"Reminds me of Alberta." Dr. MacPherson broke the silence.

Ruth jumped. Quickly gathering herself together, she quelled the sudden surge of panic she felt at the prospect of a conversation and timidly asked, "Alberta? Which part of America is that?" Pleased with herself for her efforts, she smiled at the doctor.

"It's Canada, not America!" replied Dr. MacPherson laughing. "Alberta's one of the western Canadian provinces, but I'm usually considered an American here in Africa. I'll never get used to it, though." He shook his head.

"I have heard Canada is a very beautiful place, but it must be awfully cold," ventured Ruth, more bravely this time.

"Only in the winter," he explained. "I can't tell you how many people I've met who think there is ice and snow all year-round. In summer it can get just as hot as it is here. And it even looks the same. That's why it reminds me of Alberta. Alberta has grassland like this; and with the wind blowing through the grass and the wide, blue sky shimmering with the heat, we could be in Alberta just as easily as Africa."

Ruth was amazed. "Surely you must be exaggerating!"

For a moment she had the unpleasant feeling he must be teasing her as he laughed at her surprise.

"No, it's true," he said, sweeping his eyes around the landscape. "But I will admit there are some differences. For one thing, we don't have acacia trees in Alberta, nor do we have huge herds of animals grazing on the plains. There were enormous herds of buffalo in years gone by, but they are gone now.

"Maybe it's the vastness of Africa that reminds me of Alberta," he went on. "The wind roaming over the wide-open plains and the immensity of the sky. Even in the deep of winter, there is the same feeling of immensity and vastness that you get here."

"I can't imagine what winter must be like," Ruth said, almost to herself, but Dr. MacPherson answered her quickly. He seemed pleased to talk about his faraway home in Alberta.

"The thing I miss most about winter is how beautiful it is. Of course it can get cold—so cold you can't even take a breath without your lungs hurting. But, on those mornings when everything is frozen solid, there is a deep, deep silence that chills you as much as the air does. Every now and then you hear a crack from the trees, or down at the lake at the bottom of our field you can hear the ice creaking and shifting. The stream that runs into the lake sometimes freezes into the shape of rapids and waterfalls making icy castles, whole cities of them, wherever the stream splashes over the rocks."

Ruth stared out to the horizon rolling heavily in the noon-day heat and tried to imagine the ice castles crackling in the quiet, cold air. But her horizons hemmed her in. She couldn't see beyond this walled African garden.

He went on, "I miss the beauty of winter, even though Africa is so wild and so much more exciting than even I imagined. But there is nothing quite like winter."

"I would like to see winter for myself one day," she ventured timidly, "but I don't suppose I ever will. My life is here on the farm with Father." She glanced worriedly over her shoulder. He was dozing uncomfortably, wincing with each bump of the car.

"I'm sorry we can't get there any faster," Dr. MacPherson said. "Your poor father is having a pretty difficult time of it."

Ruth looked at him in surprise. "Why, we are going faster than I have ever been in my whole life!" she exclaimed.

Dr. MacPherson threw back his head and laughed. "Well, it is certainly a rare privilege to take a girl out for her first ride in a motorcar. I must confess that I have been very remiss in my manners. "Miss Jones, I'd like to introduce you to Wild Rose, Rosie, to her friends." He tapped the dashboard in front of Ruth and grinned proudly. "Rosie is named after the wild roses that grow everywhere in Alberta. Even though Rosie and I made each other's acquaintance in Nairobi, I figured she needed a good Canadian name if we were going to be partners."

Ruth was beginning to relax in Dr. MacPherson's company. Perhaps it was the American familiarity with which he spoke to her. It was as if he just assumed they were friends. She liked it and it made her bolder. "I hear you are trying to build your hospital in Campbellburgh," she said. "What brought you to Africa all the way from Canada?"

He shot a quick glance over to her. "So you have heard about my difficulties with the local aristocracy, have you?"

"Oh no, not really." Ruth was suddenly afraid to offend him. "Florence Campbell is my aunt, that's all. Her daughter Annie is my friend and she just mentioned it briefly, but I really don't know anything about it."

Dr. MacPherson chuckled mischievously. "So you are a blood relation of the formidable Lady Campbell, are you? I'd better be on my guard, then. She has her spies everywhere!"

"Oh no, not me!" Ruth spoke quickly. "Aunt Florence doesn't approve of me at all. She would never discuss business with me." She had a sudden urge to make it quite clear to Dr. MacPherson that she was not on Florence's side. She wanted him to like her. She rattled on, "I think a hospital in Campbellburgh is a wonderful idea. I just hope you are successful, because we do need a hospital here. I run a clinic up on the farm, and there are so many times I would send someone to a hospital if there were one close by. But to send them all the way to Nairobi is very difficult. I only do it if it is a matter of life and death." She stopped, embarrassed by her outpouring of opinion. But Dr. MacPherson smiled broadly.

"Well, thank you for your vote of support. I was beginning to think there was not one person in the entire town who had anything good to say about a hospital. They have all closed ranks against me."

Ruth looked ahead at the escarpment in the distance. It was looming larger now, and she could make out the road winding up the side. How quickly they were coming to the other side of the plains. Her father was still sleeping in the backseat. Ruth was grateful at least for that. She turned to Dr. MacPherson. "Whatever made you come to Campbellburgh to build a hospital? Surely it's not the only place in the world that needs one."

He smiled. "That's a long story, but I guess we have the time, if you really want to hear it." Ruth nodded.

"I grew up on a farm out in the middle of nowhere, like you. My mother is a very faithful Christian woman, and one day when I was about twelve or thirteen, she took me and my brothers to hear a missionary speaker who was passing through the area. A huge tent was set up in a field, and people came from all over the countryside to hear the man speak.

I was so excited by the novelty of it all that I could hardly sit still, and I still remember my mother threatening to sell me to the zoo if I didn't stop behaving like a monkey!

"Well, after a few restless minutes and a well-placed swat from my mother, I settled down and started to listen. The missionary spoke about how he had worked with Albert Schweitzer in his mission hospital in West Africa. He had a real sense of adventure and excitement in his spirit, and he told story after story of what Africa was really like. I was spellbound. Then he spoke about the need for people to hear the Gospel—people whose lives were burdened with superstition and fear of dark, unpredictable gods. And he also told of their suffering with sickness and disease and how we in more 'civilized' countries had much of the help they needed. But there was no one to go to them. They needed doctors, hospitals, and above all, Christian men and women to tell them about the Gospel so they could be set free from the dark powers that ruled their lives." He took a deep breath.

"It was then and there that I decided to be a missionary, though I confess that back then it was more likely the lure of adventure in darkest Africa, fighting against evil, not to mention lions and snakes and other fearsome creatures, that spoke to my soul rather than the pure Christian love that should have been my first motive.

"But the Lord works in mysterious ways, and my mother had always prayed that one of her children would become a missionary. So, as time went on, my motives changed and I felt the true call of God to the mission field. And remembering the old missionary at the tent meeting, I felt that medical training would be the most useful way to prepare myself to serve in a practical way as well."

Dr. MacPherson slowed the car down, and Ruth noticed that the escarpment had loomed up before them quite suddenly. The dry grasses had given way to green bushes, and they in turn were becoming trees as the road began the steep, winding climb ahead. As they started to climb upward, Ruth could feel Rosie's engine working harder. She glanced back at her father, who had awakened with the change in the sound of the motor. "Are you all right, Father?" Ruth asked.

"How much longer do I have to stay in this bouncing monkey cage?" Ruth was startled to hear him speak so clearly; but before she could reply, he had already closed his eyes and lapsed back to sleep. She turned to Dr. MacPherson with a worried look.

He smiled at her reassuringly. "It won't be long now and we'll be at the hospital. Why don't you tell me about yourself? I've been doing all the talking."

"Oh no," answered Ruth quickly, "I was so interested in your story. There's nothing to say about me. Besides, you still haven't explained why you came to Campbellburgh."

"Well, are you certain I'm not boring you?" Ruth shook her head, and he continued. "After I had finished my training, my father died and left me a small inheritance since the farm was going to my younger brothers. I spent many hours in prayer deciding what to do with the money. By this point I had made up my mind not to marry, so I felt that as I wouldn't have to support a family, I would like to invest it in the furthering of God's kingdom. Gradually I concluded that God was telling me to build a hospital in East Africa as Dr. Schweitzer had done in West Africa. Since East Africa has opened up to the European settlers with the railway, the African natives are being decimated by disease.

"I studied maps and spoke to as many people as I could find and concluded that Campbellburgh was an ideal location. First, there is no hospital facility in the area. Second, it is served by both a railroad and a river, making it accessible to Africans from a large surrounding area. Therefore, I set my sights on Campbellburgh."

"That is the very reason you are having such trouble building a hospital there then," Ruth replied. "It is also an ideal location for tourists. My uncle's hotel does a brisk business with big game hunters starting out on safari and fishermen because they can come in by rail and get just about anywhere easily from Campbellburgh. Aunt Florence thinks that too many sick Africans hanging about will ruin the quality of tourism in the town."

"Well, even if that were true, which it isn't, I don't understand why she won't let me build my hospital farther up the river. But she's got the settlers up in arms all up and down the line. And I don't want to be too far away from the railroad because I'll need supplies and all sorts of things." He paused. Ruth didn't say anything. She was too intimidated by his passionate frustration with Aunt Florence. But he spoke again a few moments later in a more composed voice. "I must just remember that it is the Lord's work I am doing, not my own. He will open the doors I need when He is ready. I tend to forget that sometimes!"

He smiled at Ruth, and she found herself smiling warmly back for an instant before she suddenly blushed and lowered her eyes to look at her rough, work-worn hands in her lap. There was a new ache in her heart suddenly, and again she remembered what she had thought driving home in the buggy after Uncle Angus's funeral. *If I were at all pretty or feminine, or even if I knew the first thing about men, like Annie does, this is the man I would choose. If there were a God like the one he and Milka seem to know so well, why, oh why, has He forgotten so completely about me?*

Rosie was laboring up the steep hillside, switching back and forth as the road wound a little higher with each turn. Then without warning, there was a screech of brakes and

Ruth was thrown forward against the dashboard. Dust billowed all around, and there was the sound of bellowing. Her father cursed loudly in the backseat.

"Elephant!" said Dr. MacPherson, already leaning over the back of his seat to help her father and make him comfortable again. Ruth pushed herself painfully away from the dashboard and turned to help him. "Came out of nowhere," he said. "Are you okay, Ruth?"

"Yes, I think so. What about you, Father, are you all right?"

But Jack only swore quietly under his breath again. He appeared to be only a weak and pale imitation of his former vigorous and intimidating self. Ruth's heart sank.

"It's all right, Ruth, he's about as well as you can expect under the circumstances." Dr. MacPherson was speaking reassuringly to her. "But we need to get him there as soon as we can." Ruth noticed a shadow of worry cross the doctor's handsome face as he looked at Jack. She knew he was doing his best. She wished they were there already. As she turned around to look ahead, she gasped with fear.

They had been silently surrounded by a herd of elephants, a river of them flowing and passing around the car as though it was nothing but a boulder tossed carelessly into their midst.

They sat quietly and waited, watching the massive shapes of elephants swaying majestically past. A familiar tingle shivered up Ruth's spine. These creatures carried a presence with them far more ancient and awesome than her small and fettered mind could conceive. The huge legs swayed like tree trunks as they went by Ruth's window, yet at the same time they were quiet and graceful. An old bull lifted his trunk and trumpeted. The earth shook with the wild, mournful noise echoing right down from the beginning of time.

"Look at the behemoth, which I made along with you."

Dr. MacPherson spoke the words aloud. A thrill of awe washed over Ruth, and her heart reached out to worship, in fear and trembling, the creator of such magnificent creatures. But the moment passed almost as suddenly as it had begun. And the elephants were still streaming past.

It was a large herd, and it took a long time passing. When the last gray shape faded silently into the bush, the world lay hushed and awed. Even the birds waited in silence. With a quick glance at Jack in the backseat, Dr. MacPherson slipped out of the car and turned the crank to start Rosie's engine. The brash, rude roar instantly made the world a smaller, tamer place again. Ruth's burden of worry about her father descended again, and they drove on, quickly and urgently climbing and climbing.

She tried to fill her mind with the memory of the elephant, as she had done after she had seen the mother and baby in the pool at the farm; but it didn't work. Fears for her father continued to intrude. She looked over at Dr. MacPherson. He was concentrating on steering Rosie around the hairpin curves and along the steep-sided roads. She wondered if he would tell her more of Canada. It was an interesting diversion.

"Please tell me more. About Canada, I mean," she asked.

As he spoke, Ruth listened, more to the sound of his voice than his actual words. She thought about him coming all the way here from Canada to build a hospital because of God. The fleeting thought crossed her mind that it would be so pleasant to be able to believe in God when people got sick and when they died. But she dismissed it quickly. She couldn't just pretend to believe something that she didn't know in her heart of hearts to be absolutely true.

They were nearing the top of the escarpment now. There were more Africans walking alongside the road, many of them women carrying huge *kikapus*, or baskets, filled with fruit and vegetables on their heads. There was a village of huts and chickens and children off to one side where the road flattened out. They had finally reached the high plain. Nairobi was not far off now. Ruth was very glad.

"When will we get there?" growled her father from the backseat. Ruth was startled by the tone of his voice. His old fierceness had disappeared completely, and there was something lifeless and empty about his voice without its passion. "If you don't get me out of this dreadful contraption soon," he complained, "you might just as well take me straight to the undertaker."

"We're just at the top of the escarpment now, Father, so it won't be long." Ruth didn't like the gray pallor of his complexion. He lapsed into silence.

Nairobi was a bigger version of Campbellburgh. The roadside quickly became crowded with people walking to and from town. The late afternoon sun reflected off the red and silver rooftops, and dust filled the air. The rows of shops had long, covered walkways in front of them. Everywhere people were selling every type of food, or shape of basket, or color of cloth you could think of. They had to push Rosie through thick flocks of totos that continually surrounded them. By the time they reached the hospital, her father was in a lot of pain. They parked Rosie at the main entrance, and Dr. MacPherson went inside to fetch a stretcher, leaving Ruth and her father to wait. He came back in a few minutes accompanied by a nurse and two stretcher bearers.

Ruth stood helplessly watching her father disappear inside the wooden green door. She tried to swallow the lump in her throat and blink away the tears in her eyes. Dr. MacPherson stepped up to her and took her by the elbow.

"Come along now, Miss Jones." He spoke soothingly and steered her up the steps. "I know the doctor who will be looking after your father, and you'll like him. Let's go inside and meet him. After you." He opened the green door, and Ruth stepped inside to be greeted by the strong smell of disinfectant.

She had been here before, but it had been many years ago and there had been a few changes since then. She wasn't sure which way to turn. Dr. MacPherson took her by the elbow again and steered her down a hall to a small green and white office. "Stephen?" he called, tapping lightly on the open door.

A young doctor looked up from the desk and stood up to greet them. He was very tall and stooped slightly as he leaned forward to shake their hands. He had pale blond, thinning hair and wore wire-rimmed glasses. His smile was warm and welcoming.

"Miss Jones, I'd like you to meet Dr. Stephen Burgess, a friend of mine. Steve, Ruth Jones. We just brought her father in from Campbellburgh with a broken thigh. His horse bolted over him. Would you look in on him for us? Miss Jones is very worried."

Dr. Burgess shook Ruth's hand. "I'm sorry about your father. But please don't worry. We'll take good care of him. My colleague, Dr. Mancini, is in the emergency room at the moment, so your father is in good hands. Come with me and we will go and see how he is doing." The three of them set off down a long corridor.

Leaving them to wait outside a large swinging door, Dr. Burgess went in to check on Jack for them. He emerged only a few minutes later with a serious expression on his face.

"I'm afraid your father must have had quite a serious fall," he said. "They are working on his leg just now. Infection has already set in, so it may be a little while before we can stabilize him and tell you exactly the extent of his injuries. Would you like to wait here? It will be a rather long wait, I'm afraid."

Dr. MacPherson spoke up. "We haven't had anything to

eat since breakfast this morning, so I think I'll just take Miss Jones to the Lord Stanley, if that is all right by her?" He looked inquiringly at Ruth and she blushed crimson.

"Oh, you can't possibly. . .I've never been in a. . .I mean, I haven't brought any money with me," she stammered helplessly.

"Oh nonsense!" breezed Dr. MacPherson, leading her back down the hall followed by Dr. Burgess. "Supper's on me! Come along!" Ruth was swept along to the front doors. Dr. MacPherson turned and thanked Dr. Burgess, and Ruth shook his hand and thanked him again. In a moment they were back in Rosie and heading off to the Lord Stanley.

"I can't possibly go to supper in a. . .a. . ." Ruth spluttered nervously. "It's just that I'm not dressed and I've never. . ."

"Oh, don't be silly," said Dr. MacPherson firmly. "We haven't had a bite since we left the farm this morning. Surely you must at least be thirsty?"

When they arrived at the hotel, a group of cool, crisply dressed women stepped smartly up the steps in high heels and silk stockings. They were chattering and laughing like the birds in the trees back home, and Ruth wished she had never left her farm. She looked down at her wrinkled khaki trousers.

"I can't possibly go in there dressed like this. I'm dressed for work."

Dr. MacPherson turned to look at Ruth as if it were the first time he had seen her. "Well, as far as I'm concerned, being dressed for work is nothing to be ashamed of. You are clean and tidy, and I for one am proud to be dining with a woman who is dressed to work. Come along, I'm starving, and I'll bet you are, too." He jumped out of the car and escorted Ruth proudly up the steps.

They were seated at a table in the corner and Ruth had her back to the rest of the patrons. She was glad. The room was dark and cool and quiet, but Ruth couldn't shake the feeling that everyone in the restaurant was looking and laughing at her, a country bumpkin who came to the Lord Stanley Hotel in work clothes. Dr. MacPherson chatted so easily she longed for self-confidence to match his.

Gradually, she began to relax a little as Dr. MacPherson explained what was good to eat and what wasn't. She asked him to order for her, embarrassed again, in case she chose something too expensive. He cheerfully ordered some chicken for both of them and leaned forward to speak to Ruth. She felt herself enveloped in his warmth and enthusiasm. His eyes caught hers, and he lowered his normally loud voice to suit the quietness of the place.

"Tell me about your life, Ruth, if I may call you that. I don't stand much on formality, so please call me Douglas." Ruth blushed hotly again at the very idea of actually being familiar enough to call him by his first name, but he pretended not to notice. "We've spent all morning talking about me, now I think it only fair that you get a turn, too. So go ahead, tell me about yourself." He sat comfortably back in the large mahogany and zebra-hide chair and waited expectantly for her to begin.

It was the first time in Ruth's entire life that anyone had ever asked her about herself. But what could she possibly tell him? When she thought about herself, there was really nothing there. "There's nothing to tell you," she stammered. "I have a pretty quiet life, just running the farm with my father."

"Ha!" Douglas let out a loud guffaw and banged his fist on the table, utterly forgetting his restaurant voice. "Ruth! Don't tell me that I have come all the way from Alberta, Canada, to have lunch with a lady who, people say, pretty much single-handedly runs a farm in the middle of Africa, and she tells me she has a quiet, boring life, like some sort of spinster aunt living with her cats and knitting woolen booties all day long! Tell me another one!" He laughed his loud, merry laugh, and Ruth felt the eyes of everyone in the restaurant searing into her back. Just to keep him quiet, she thought she'd better come up with something.

"Well," she began slowly, hoping the darkness of the room would hide the redness of her face, "my mother died when I was little, and as soon as my father felt I had had enough schooling, he taught me how to farm. It is really the only life I know. We grow quite a bit of coffee, and we also have a herd of dairy cows." She told him about the intricacies of growing coffee and of the weather and the cows and the difficulties of finding good help. Finally, the waiter brought the chicken, and Ruth stopped talking, grateful for the interruption.

Ruth was indeed starving, and she tucked into the chicken with relish. It tasted delicious; and when she was nearly finished, she stopped eating so quickly and made a conscious effort to savor the rest of the meal. Douglas laughed when he saw her pause.

"You really were hungry, weren't you?"

Ruth nodded, her mouth full. "It's delicious," she mumbled gratefully. "Our cook doesn't make chicken like this!"

"I'm glad you're enjoying it so much. I don't imagine you get much chance to get out, living way up where you do."

Ruth took another bite and shook her head.

"It must be quite lonely for you, with just your father to talk to," he continued.

Ruth swallowed her mouthful. He was sounding suspiciously like he was becoming sorry for her. Not a genuine sorrow, but a sort of patronizing pity that she had come to recognize in people's voices when they spoke to her, as though she couldn't be treated quite as an equal. She loathed it. Once Douglas succumbed to it, he would never come out of it. Of course, it was bound to happen sooner or later. There was, after all, no one who didn't come to that conclusion about her eventually. But not today, not yet.

"I actually am not a bit lonely," she protested. "I'm far too busy. And Milka, the cook, has been a mother to me. I couldn't have asked for anyone nicer, really." Ruth realized she was talking too quickly. She took a deep breath. "I also have a very good friend, Annie Campbell. I think you know her. So really my life is not the slightest bit lonely."

Douglas quickly responded, "I'm sorry, Ruth. I didn't mean to offend you. I guess I just thought that running a farm so far away from town with only your father, it must be a little isolating. Of course you have friends. I did meet Annie. She is a very nice person, though to be absolutely honest, I can't say the same for her mother!" He chuckled ruefully.

"By the way, I was wondering whether you are planning to stay here in Nairobi. I would be very happy to lend you a little cash if you want to stay at the hotel." Douglas had resumed a more businesslike voice. "I have to stay myself, so I will be able to drive you over to the hospital in the morning."

"Oh, my goodness," Ruth panicked. "I can't possibly stay. I haven't told Milka or Kamau. I can't leave Father alone here, either. Oh dear, but I ought to be at home."

"Well, we can go back and see how your father is. Then, if you want to go home tonight, you can catch the overnight train and you will be in Campbellburgh in the morning. I would be able to look in on your father tomorrow for you. I shouldn't think there is much you'll be able to do for him until he is feeling a little better. You may as well go home and straighten out things and then come back when you can stay a few days.

"My cousin Alex arrives by train tomorrow night, so I won't be back in Campbellburgh for a couple of days. I can keep an eye on your father for you while I'm here, and I'll bring you news when I get back."

"Thank you!" Ruth sighed gratefully. The thought of spending an entire night here in Nairobi sent her into a flat spin. Douglas could look after Father now and she would return later. "Would you give me a lift to the station after we go to the hospital then?" She still hadn't found the courage to use his first name, but she managed to bite her tongue before she called him Dr. MacPherson again.

Douglas reached for the check. "Of course."

&

Back at the hospital, Ruth found Jack newly installed in a ward, his leg in a huge cast that effectively pinned him to the bed.

"Hello, Father," she whispered, pulling aside the curtain just enough to let herself in. He greeted her with an angry growl, like a cornered animal facing its attacker. She felt hot tears rushing to her eyes. He didn't belong here. *What have I done to him?* He looked so out of place wearing a green hospital gown that revealed a strip of white flesh on his neck where his collar always covered the sun. It was indecent. She had an overwhelming urge to get him out of bed and take him home as fast as she could. She suddenly wanted everything to go back to the way it always was. It was too painful to see him like this.

With a shaking voice, she asked, "Have they been treating you well, Father?"

"They might as well just take me out back and shoot me. It would save everyone a lot of trouble."

Ruth tried another tack. "Is your leg feeling better with the cast on?"

Jack snorted with derision, and otherwise deigned not

to reply. Footsteps sounded in the hall, and Dr. Burgess walked in.

"Hello, Miss Jones." Dr. Burgess stood on the other side of the bed. "I have a couple of things to discuss with you."

"I have already spoken to Mr. Jones about this, Miss Jones. I would like him to stay here for at least a month. Despite the pain killers we have given him, he will still be in considerable pain with the fracture in his leg and the infection. But what I am more concerned about is his high blood pressure. I would like to do a few tests to see if we can discover the cause of it." He patted Jack consolingly on his arm. "I know it is an inconvenience, but I wouldn't want you returning home unless you were well enough for your daughter to look after, and I am afraid that is just not the case at the moment." He smiled at Ruth, ignoring Jack's angry snort. He put out his hand and Ruth shook it, then he vanished quickly out of the curtain. Ruth was left looking desperately at Jack, who deliberately closed his eyes.

"I am sorry, Father," she whispered sadly. There was no response. "I will come back and visit as soon as I can, and don't worry about the farm. I will take good care of everything, just the way you would."

Jack opened his eyes, and Ruth was shocked to see a cold, calm fury glaring out at her. There was a sickening pain filling her stomach as she looked at him.

"You will go home now and stay there." He was speaking with deliberate, controlled rage at her. "You will not come back here. I don't want to see you. Now get out." Ruth stared, paralyzed with horror and disbelief.

"Father. . ." she whispered at last.

"You've had your way. You brought me here, now get out!" he hissed.

She turned and fled through the curtain. She wouldn't see him again at the hospital. She may as well take the train home tonight. She began to shake as she walked down the echoing corridor.

Douglas was waiting for her at the end of the hall. "How is he?" he asked, looking at Ruth with careful concern.

He must know that my father hates me, thought Ruth irrationally. "Not very well, I'm afraid," she replied in a shaken voice.

Douglas put his arm around her shoulders and helped her into the car. They drove quickly to the station and bought Ruth a ticket for the train. People were busily milling about. Everyone seemed to know just where they were going. Ruth felt lost. She was confused. The rage in her father's face blocked out all rational thought. She just wanted to be alone. Douglas steered her to a train car. She turned to say goodbye at the steps, but to her horror, when she tried to speak, tears filled her eyes and she stood speechless.

Impulsively, Douglas reached forward and gave her a quick hug. "Good-bye, Ruth. I'll be seeing you."

"Good-bye, Douglas," she whispered back before she turned and fled up the steps.

five

Early in the morning two days later, Ruth nervously mounted Chui and set out on the dusty road down the hillside, making for Jimmy MacRae's farm. She hated the thought of leaving home in case Douglas brought her news of her father, but she had to help Annie. The last days had been intensely long and horribly lonely. She hadn't wanted to tell anyone that her father refused to see her. It was shameful.

She had caught herself in the depths of her loneliness, longing to see Douglas MacPherson's face again. She wanted to talk to him once more and feel the same warm familiarity that his presence brought to her. She remembered over and over again the sound of his voice, the shape of his mouth, and the sparkle of his blue eyes. For two days now she had been riding through the hot, dusty fields, checking on the bibis toiling in the dry soil. But her eyes were really seeing lovely, intricate castles made of sparkling ice, set in shimmering lacy forests where she and Douglas walked and talked and laughed together. The memory of her father lying sick and broken in the hospital in Nairobi, which always brought a sick stone of pain crashing into the pit of her stomach, faded as she thought of Douglas. Oh, how she didn't want to leave the farm in case he came. But Annie's pleading face also intruded into her mind, so Ruth decided to get up early and visit Jimmy MacRae. She had to do something to help. She couldn't let Annie down—not Annie, of all people.

As Ruth rode out onto the plain, the silver roofs of Campbellburgh were glinting in the rapidly warming sunshine.

She was hot. She hoped Jimmy was at the farm and wished the MacRae farm were on the same side of town as hers. The ride across the plain seemed to have become longer and harder than she ever remembered it before. Even the ugly old baobab didn't capture Ruth's imagination the way it usually did, and she passed it by with barely a glance. Just before reaching Campbellburgh, she turned south.

The MacRae farm was much smaller than theirs. As she rode up the driveway, chickens and ducks scurried out from under Chui's feet with indignant cackles as if to demand why a mere horse should have right-of-way. A couple of goats contentedly munched on dry grass inside a small boma off to one side, and some totos sat on the fence in front of them, waving cheerfully at Ruth as if they were playing a game of trying to make her wave back. She did.

The house was small and old and had a thatched roof and no lawn or flowers in the front. Ruth was ashamed to find herself feeling a degree of understanding for Florence's dislike of having Jimmy MacRae for a son-in-law. It would certainly be a terrific blow to the Campbell pride to have one of their daughters marry into such a lowly situation. But when Jimmy himself came striding purposefully from around the back of the house, his hands dirty and his black hair plastered down with sweat and a broad, welcoming smile on his face, Ruth smiled back rather sheepishly. Annie was right—he was a good man.

"Good morning to you, Ruth Jones," he shouted cheerily. "What can I do for you this morning?"

Ruth jumped lightly down from Chui. Jimmy was not terribly tall, and he had a wiry build. Ruth could look him directly in the eyes. She realized with surprise that it had been a very long time since she had actually seen him, let alone spoken to him. He was friendlier than she remembered. She came straight to the point.

"I'm here to bring you a message from Annie." She was touched to see his face immediately light up from the inside. "But it's not very good news."

"Is she all right?" Jimmy's light faded as suddenly as it had appeared.

"I think so. I had lunch with her a couple of days ago. She is quite depressed. She is worried that you may feel that she too easily gave in to her mother's wishes not to marry you. At the same time she is afraid of disobeying her mother. And her mother will allow her no visitors or correspondence in case she is secretly getting in touch with you."

"I must do something!" Jimmy's voice was quiet with worry. He shielded his hand across his eyes. "I'm sorry I couldn't come sooner," Ruth said. "My father had an accident and I had to take him to the hospital in Nairobi."

"I am so sorry to hear that! I hope it was not too serious." Jimmy remembered his manners quickly, but Ruth could tell his mind was only on Annie, so she merely nodded and went on.

"I will call on my aunt to tell her about my father's accident. I will try to pass a message to Annie from you if you would like."

Jimmy brightened again. "Oh, thank you very much, Miss Jones. I would be very grateful to you. Please excuse my terrible manners and come inside for a glass of orange or lemon squash!" He led the way onto the little, bare veranda and opened the front door for Ruth. "Perhaps we can even have an early lunch. I so rarely have visitors, but I'll go and see what the cook has. Excuse me for just a moment."

While Ruth's eyes were still adjusting from the glaring midday sun, he slipped away through a door on the far side of the room. Ruth stood awkwardly by the door and looked around. There was one large, well-worn, burgundy brocade armchair next to a rough stone fireplace. The table next to the chair contained a huge, equally worn, open Bible. Over the fireplace mantle, Jimmy had placed a wooden cross instead of the usual hunting trophies. The two pieces of wood were bound with string and unpolished.

Otherwise, there was very little else in the room. A real bachelor's home, Ruth thought. Annie would have the place cozy and inviting in no time. Jimmy returned carrying a tray of glasses and a jug of squash, which he set on top of the Bible.

"Sorry to keep you waiting." He pulled out a couple of chairs that Ruth hadn't noticed behind the door and carried them outside onto the veranda. Ruth picked up the tray and followed him outside. He took it from her and balanced it on the veranda railing. They sat down.

"You know, Florence Campbell is right," Jimmy began. "Annie does deserve a husband who can provide all the finer things in life for her. I know I don't have very much at the moment, but I work hard; and if I could just have a bit of time, I'll be able to provide Annie with the kind of life she deserves. And Annie says she'll wait for me." Poor Jimmy. He sounds so hopeful. Ruth wanted to say something comforting.

"I'm sure that Florence will relent soon. After all, Uncle Angus's death is so recent. After she recovers a little more, she will begin to see that you and Annie are truly in love, and then she will give her consent."

"Thank you, Ruth. I hope you are right." Ruth felt Jimmy's eyes looking gratefully toward her, and she blushed.

There was a small silence, and Ruth heard the soft padding of footsteps in the house behind her. The door opened, and a very tall man came out, carrying a tray of cold roast beef and a jellied salad.

"Thank you, Karioke," said Jimmy as Karioke set the tray down on the veranda railing next to the drinks. "You will join me for lunch, Miss Jones? I'm afraid it isn't much, but we can eat on our laps, if you don't mind."

"No, not at all," Ruth replied as Karioke passed her a clean, but chipped plate and a tin knife and fork.

While they ate, Jimmy politely questioned Ruth about her farm, and they discussed the price of milk and coffee. Afterward, Karioke came and took away their plates and brought them each a cup of coffee.

Jimmy turned to Ruth. "Would you mind if I left you for a moment while I just write a note for you to give to Annie?" She nodded and he went inside, returning a short while later with an envelope.

"Thank you, again, Miss Jones. This means so much to us both." He smiled at her with deep gratitude.

"It is a pleasure," replied Ruth, wishing he wouldn't call her Miss Jones. She held out her hand. Jimmy shook it. She ran down the steps, untied Chui, and waved good-bye as she cantered down the road. She turned back once to see Jimmy standing forlornly, watching her go. Poor Jimmy.

Just on the outskirts of town, Ruth pulled Chui up for a minute on a little knoll that overlooked the river and the town of Campbellburgh on the far side. She looked right across the river from the church where Angus Campbell's funeral had been. And there, next to it, lay the empty plot of land that had belonged to her mother, spreading down toward the river. She wondered if her father would ever use it for anything. Her parents had once thought of building a house and retiring there, at least her mother had; but her father would never be content so surrounded by civilization.

Ruth let Chui graze half-heartedly in the dry grass by the road. She jumped down, threw the reins over a little bush, and walked down to the banks of the river. Her mother's land was mostly dry scrub, but there was a green bank of lush bush along the riverbank. It was a lovely, serene spot.

Ruth wondered what Florence had told her father about the possibility of selling it to Douglas MacPherson for his hospital. She would no doubt exercise her right of first refusal if he tried.

She made a quick stop at the Campbells', and in the shock at the news of her father, she managed to slip Jimmy's note to Annie without being seen. Then she rode back up to the farm on the hill in the heat of the afternoon. She had so much to think over that she didn't really notice how hot it had been until she reached the little river valley.

The cool air welcomed her home like an old, beloved friend, refreshing and relaxing her with just its very presence. The winding track led her along the still waters of the pools and the musical rapids bubbling between them. A feeling came over Ruth that the foundations of her life were imperceptibly, but irrevocably beginning to shift. *Perhaps it's just the worry of Father in the hospital,* she thought, shrugging the feeling away. A cool wind blew past her face and rustled the trees behind her on its way down through the valley. *There is freedom in the wind,* Ruth thought.

As she walked up the path from the stable, the low growl of a motor gradually began to imprint itself onto Ruth's consciousness. She looked up quickly. Sure enough, a smudge of dust was rising up from the side of the hill. Ruth pushed her hat back on her head and walked faster to reach the house before the motorcar arrived. She noticed rather sheepishly that her cheeks were flushed with excitement. Soon she would see Douglas again. But she also felt a flutter of apprehension as she wondered what news he was bringing of her father. She pulled her hat back down over her eyes to hide the telltale signs of her excitement and worry.

Rosie emerged from the valley just as Ruth hurried onto the veranda to look for her. She squinted into the glare of the afternoon sun behind the car. She suddenly realized that she was hot and perspiring. Her face was likely streaked with dust, and her shirt was damp and dirty. Quickly, she turned and fled inside. Running lightly down the hall to her bedroom, she found the washbasin in her room already filled for her. Splashing her face quickly, she pulled off her old shirt and threw a clean white one over her head. She was just tucking it into her trousers when she heard voices in the lounge and Milka's footsteps padding down the hall to find her. She reached for her brush, pulled it two or three times through her hair, and opened her door to tell Milka she was coming.

The flutter of excitement that had carried her through the last few moments, suddenly dropped like a stone down into the pit of her stomach. What news was Douglas bringing her of her father? Surely she wasn't so callous as to be worrying about the impression she was trying to make on a man, rather than considering her father's health. Feeling guilty, she ducked past the glaring animal eyes above her and went quickly down the hall. Nervously, she burst into the lounge and stopped short.

"Good afternoon, Ruth," came Douglas's cheerful voice as he stepped forward to shake her hand. "I just thought I'd run up to bring you news of your father." But Ruth stared past him. There was another man standing behind him. Noticing her look, Douglas turned to the man. "I'd like you to meet my cousin Alex. Ruth, Alex Kendall. Alex, Ruth Jones."

The man stepped up to Ruth and they exchanged polite greetings. Alex Kendall was a thin, dark-haired man, elegantly dressed, complete with a silk shirt and a red ascot around his neck. He had a pencil-thin mustache and a quick flash of a smile. Ruth thought he was rather formally dressed for a visit to a farm.

"Alex arrived in Nairobi last evening," Douglas said, and

Ruth turned her attention back to him.

I'd forgotten how warm his smile is and how kind his eyes are, she thought as he looked up into his face, trying to remember every nuance of his presence to savor later.

"Miss Jones," Alex interrupted her thought. His voice was smooth and confidant. "This is certainly a lovely location you have here for your farm. Douglas tells me you run the place single-handedly."

Ruth quickly glanced at him. His eyes were the same piercing blue as Douglas's, but they weren't brimming with merriment like his cousin's. They seemed almost expressionless, with maybe a hint of calculation underneath. Douglas was already starting to tell Ruth how her father was.

"I dropped in at the hospital this morning before we left Nairobi. I didn't actually see your father, since I didn't want to upset him, but I spoke with Dr. Burgess. His thigh is pretty badly broken, but given time it will heal, even at his age." Ruth smiled hopefully at this news, but Douglas's face became more serious.

"Unfortunately, there seems to be something wrong with his liver, and Dr. Burgess is running some tests to try to determine exactly what it is. He thinks it will be quite a while before your dad will be able to leave the hospital. But he wanted me to assure you that Mr. Jones is doing as well as can be expected under the circumstances. He is, of course, a little angry at being confined to bed and, as a result, is not always the most cooperative of patients. But the nurses are used to handling all sorts of people, so not to worry. Dr. Burgess says you need not rush back to Nairobi until you are quite ready. Your father is in very capable hands."

"Something's wrong with his liver?" Ruth echoed, remembering the weight of worry that she had felt earlier. Her shoulders slumped and she felt blood draining out of her face.

Douglas quickly stepped up and put his arm around her shoulder.

"Here, Ruth, sit down." He helped her to the nearest chair. "Now you really mustn't worry about your father. Dr. Burgess is an excellent physician, and he won't let anything happen to him. Perhaps it is providential that he had this accident, although I don't want to make any excuses for my driving. But if there is something the matter, we will be able to nip it in the bud. I'm sure your father will be up and about just as soon as humanly possible. Come now, I'll go and find us all a cup of tea. Look after her, Alex, will you?" Douglas went out through the door into the hall, and she could hear him calling *"Jambo, jambo!"* as he looked for the kitchen.

Alex Kendall sat on a chair near Ruth's. "I'm most terribly sorry about your father," he said politely.

"Thank you," Ruth replied, wishing he would go away. She couldn't think of a single thing to say to him. They sat for a few minutes in uncomfortable silence until the sound of Douglas's footsteps could be heard coming down the hall.

"I found Milka in the kitchen," he said coming in and sitting beside Ruth. "She'll be here with a cup of tea for us in a moment." Ruth smiled up at him gratefully. She was even more grateful when he chatted with Alex about the kind of farming that they did in this part of Africa and the type of hunting and fishing in the area.

Milka came in with the tea and cake and scones and bustled about, serving everyone. Ruth sipped hers thankfully and listened as Douglas teased Milka about luring her away from her job as Ruth's cook to come and work for him. Milka giggled and demurred, half embarrassed and half pleased. It was unusual to have a visitor pay any attention to her. Ruth glanced over at Alex. He was looking on rather disapprovingly, she thought, his long fingers curling around his teacup like tentacles.

Milka set the teapot down on the table next to Ruth. "Will the bwanas be staying for dinner?" she asked Ruth pointedly.

"Oh, I don't know," Ruth stammered, panicking at the thought of entertaining two gentlemen alone. At least she wouldn't have minded if it were only Douglas, but his cousin was rather haughty. Well, there was no polite way out of it. Milka was standing in front of her waiting for an answer.

"Please, won't you join me for dinner," Ruth said quickly turning to Douglas. "I usually have quite a plain one, but I would be so glad to have you both stay."

"Thank you most kindly, but we really must be getting back to town. Alex is still tired from his journey and he needs an early night. Perhaps another time when we have more time we'll take you up on your offer." Douglas spoke quickly and firmly. Ruth felt relieved. It had been a long day for her, too, and she just wanted to crawl into bed and worry about her father. Maybe if it had been Douglas alone. . .

But Alex was speaking to her. "While I am here, I would very much like to take a safari and do some big game hunting. Do you know anyone who does that sort of thing in Campbellburgh?"

"Oh, yes," Ruth replied. "That is easy to find in Campbellburgh. There is a white hunter named Terry Matthews, who works for Angus Campbell. He regularly takes tourists out on safari. You just need to inquire at the Campbell Arms Hotel."

"Oh good, I'll do that. We are staying at the Campbell Arms."

They chatted easily now about big game and the various hunting grounds in the area. Ruth asked Douglas if he was going on safari also, but before he could reply, a snort of laughter came from Alex. Ruth turned to him in surprise.

"Our Douglas doesn't hunt, Miss Jones," Alex said condescendingly. "He saves lives, not destroys them! Have you not heard he is planning to build a hospital in Campbellburgh?"

"Yes, I have," Ruth answered, feeling brave with annoyance at his tone of voice. "I am very glad of it. The Africans in the area are in serious need of a hospital they can reach quickly and easily."

"Well, they've survived nicely for centuries," Alex replied. "It hardly seems worthwhile to go to such trouble and expense when they have their own methods of dealing with sickness. Probably they're just as effective as ours when all's said and done."

"Alex, one day's sojourn here in Campbellburgh hardly qualifies you to judge whether or not the native population would benefit from a hospital." There was a distinct note of irritation in Douglas's voice as he responded to his cousin.

Alex laughed cheerily. "Well, well, Doug, my boy, there is no need to be so serious about it all. After all, we didn't come here for Miss Jones to hear us argue about the merits of medical missionaries. Besides, it doesn't look as though anything will come of your plans if you can't even get these Campbells to sell you one small plot." Alex sat back smugly, having had the last word, so he thought.

"I'm not done with the Campbells yet, Alex." Then he turned to Ruth. "Thank you so much for the tea, Ruth, but we really must be on our way." He shot a significant glare at Alex as he spoke.

Then smiling kindly, he went on, "Your father will be as right as rain when Dr. Burgess has finished with him, so please don't allow yourself to worry needlessly over him."

"Thank you for your kindness," answered Ruth, wishing with all her heart there was some small way she could tell him how much his kindness had meant to her over the last few days.

Ruth saw them off at the veranda and stood watching as Rosie headed down the hillside, her cloud of dust trailing gaily behind her. She was not sorry to see the last of Alex, but she wished that she had been able to have Douglas to herself again. Their trip to Nairobi together already seemed like an old, old dream. She slowly turned to go inside the quiet, empty house.

Milka was in the lounge collecting the tea tray.

"I have heard about the *bwana*." Milka's voice sounded hushed with impending tragedy as she turned to speak to Ruth. "I fear he will not return to us. That hospital cannot cure what it is that is making him ill."

"Oh, Milka, you are speaking nonsense again." Ruth spoke harshly despite the pang of fear that Milka's words sent into her heart. "How can you possibly know anything about the *bwana*? He is in the hospital in Nairobi under the care of a very good *daktari*. Daktari MacPherson said so himself!"

Milka ignored her speech and continued in a portentous tone, "I pray that God will perform a miracle for him, just as he is doing for you." She walked out the door into the hallway.

Ruth followed her, despite herself. What was Milka going on about now? Miracles and such nonsense. Humph.

Milka set the tea tray in the kitchen and demanded her hapless toto wash them up instantly. Ruth sat down at the table.

"Now, the new American, Daktari MacPherson, he is a fine man. I can see it just by looking at him. He likes you very much, too." Milka smiled conspiratorially to Ruth.

"Milka!" Ruth retorted. "What are you getting at? Dr. MacPherson is not interested in me. He is not interested in anybody. He told me so himself!" Milka just raised her eyebrows and looked down her nose at Ruth with a knowing smile.

"Just stop it, Milka!" Ruth felt her cheeks getting redder by the second, and she simmered with frustration at herself, at Milka, at her life. "Douglas MacPherson is not going to marry anybody. Even if he were, I'm sure I would be the last person he would choose. He is a kind person, that is all there is to it!"

How did Milka know everything about me and Douglas and about Father, too? Really, she was getting far too big for her boots, Ruth fumed. She could tell that Milka was smiling, even though she had her back turned and was reaching up to put away some of the china that the toto had finished washing. Ruth stood up.

"Well, I'm tired!" She picked up her hat and stalked out of the door.

Ruth went straight to her bedroom and threw herself onto her bed.

How could Milka be so frustrating? But it was true. Milka was right; she wanted Douglas MacPherson. She wanted to be with him and knew it now. Absolutely, without a shadow of a doubt. And without a shadow of a doubt, she also knew that she would never have him. Her dreams of joy shattered like glass the moment she dreamed them.

She glared out of her window into the quickly darkening evening. The colors of the treetops were gray and cold. The sky itself was neither blue nor black, but some empty, colorless vacuum. Ruth felt gray and dead inside. How could Milka be so unkind as to talk that way about Douglas when there wasn't a hope in heaven of anything coming of it?

And what about Father? What would I do here forever and ever without him? It is too soon for him to die. He couldn't go just yet, I'm not ready. Surely Douglas was right, he would be right as rain soon. Douglas had to be right. He had to be.

A heart-shattering sob exploded out of her breast and hot tears burst out onto her cheeks. She buried her head in her pillow and sobbed like a baby. No, she thought, no baby ever had a heart hard enough to break like this. She wept for fear of being alone. She wept because of her father. She wept because of Douglas.

And when Ruth finally became quiet, everything was the same as it had ever been. Everything except her. She wanted life, a life of her own. She smiled grimly. She had no idea how to even begin to live her own life. She was poor, plain, tall, and utterly alone. Standing over by her window now, she looked out into the vast, empty sky. Even the stars were still few and far between. For the first time since the old, old days of her childhood, she uttered a prayer out loud, sending it soaring out of the darkness of her bedroom, soaring out beyond the darkness of the night outside.

"Please, God," she begged, "I want to live. I want to marry Douglas MacPherson and live. You made me a living woman, and I want, somehow, no matter how hopeless it is, to at least try to be alive before I die."

And just for a moment, she was acutely aware that she had now done everything she could, and the rest would have to be up to God, if He was there, if He cared. She was helpless.

six

Early in the morning, a week later, Ruth received word that her Aunt Florence would be making a visit to Ruth to comfort her in the time of her father's illness. The news set Milka into a flurry of baking and cleaning, and Ruth went to her bedroom to change into her tweed skirt. Only after she opened her closet did she remember what she had done to it. She stood staring into the empty darkness with mingled relief and guilt. She could wear the only other dress she owned, her black funeral one, but that would mean fixing the tear on the side. Besides, the black dress was even hotter and more uncomfortable than the tweed skirt. Florence would be expecting her to be in a dress, like a well-brought-up Christian girl. She sat on her bed to think the matter out.

This was absolutely ridiculous, she decided. Here she was, a thirty-two-year-old woman, and she didn't even own a proper dress in which to receive visitors. Surely she and her father weren't that poor! But her father always handled all their money, and she was only given a very small allowance to buy certain necessities. The only clothes her father approved for her were men's trousers and shirts.

She had gradually become aware this week that she would have to go into town to see the bank about the money. Each morning she collected the milk money and put it in the cash box in her father's office. He took it into the bank once a month and deposited it, complaining bitterly about what a pitiful amount it was and how difficult it was for an honest farmer to eke out a living these days. It had been the same ever since Ruth could remember.

But for now, as she sat staring into her empty closet, she decided at last that she would face Aunt Florence in her cleanest trousers and white shirt. Then, before her father came back from the hospital, she would go to town and have Mrs. Singh, the dressmaker, sew her a dress. When her father saw it, she would just explain that her old clothes didn't fit anymore. There would be nothing he could do then. She shuddered in fear at making her father angry, but she resolved in her mind that it was time she had at least one plain dress.

Florence's buggy sailed up to the farmhouse at precisely three o'clock. As usual, Ruth awaited her arrival on the veranda. Today, much to her astonishment, not only were Aunt Florence and Annie in the carriage, so was Alex Kendall! Ruth stood and stared as Alex jumped out and handed first Aunt Florence down and then Annie. *Annie looks tired and thin,* Ruth thought, as she saw Annie quickly let go of Alex's hand after she reached the ground.

Aunt Florence had surged up the steps to Ruth then stopped short in front of her. "Good Lord, Ruth Jones, your poor father goes into the hospital and not two weeks later you are receiving visitors in khaki trousers, like some sort of bush farmer who knows no better! Your mother will be turning over in her grave at the very thought. How could you do such a thing! And we have Mr. Kendall here, too. I was so hoping you would make a favorable impression on him, you know, for the sake of the family! We don't want him thinking we are utterly uncivilized out here, even if we have to reside in darkest Africa!"

She turned toward Alex and Annie, who had followed her up the steps, and laughed a high-pitched, apologetic little giggle for Alex's benefit and continued her monologue. "As I told you, my dear Mr. Kendall, Ruth is one of the less accomplished of the Campbell girls, but her dear mother was a saint. It is because of her mother that I have taken it upon myself to see to it that her father brings her up in a proper Christian manner!" She swept a withering look at her niece and stepped majestically aside.

"Miss Ruth Jones, may I present Mr. Alex Kendall. Mr. Kendall, Miss Jones."

Alex stepped forward and bowed slightly in Ruth's direction. Turning to Florence he said, "Mrs. Campbell, Miss Jones and I have already had the pleasure of being introduced."

Complete shock actually struck Florence dumb for a moment. Alex seized his opportunity. "I came to see Miss Jones with my cousin, Dr. MacPherson, on the first day that I arrived in Campbellburgh in order to bring her news of her father's condition."

Florence recovered quickly. "I see," she said coldly, eyeing Ruth. "You do not waste much time in meeting the eligible young men in town, do you? I hear you even persuaded our Dr. MacPherson into driving you and your father all the way to Nairobi."

Ruth turned crimson with shame and embarrassment. "I. . .he just. . .I mean it's not like that at all," she stammered and stumbled over her words. Annie rushed to her rescue.

"Mother! How could you say such a terrible thing about Ruth? When has she ever behaved like that in her entire life? Honestly, Mother, how could you!"

Florence was slightly taken aback at the strange outburst from her usually obedient daughter, but she wasn't going to be put in the wrong. "You are very young, my dear, and obviously you know very little about the ways of the world. Women of a certain age can become desperate in affairs of the heart. One can never be too careful, you know."

Ruth was utterly appalled at the turn the conversation was taking, and they hadn't even gone inside the house yet. Aunt Florence must have read her mind because she suddenly set sail for the door and swept through it.

Milka was just setting out a tray of tea things on the table. Florence descended on the table with relish, poured herself a cup of tea, and loaded her plate with the cakes and scones that Milka had baked for the occasion. Taking a huge helping of whipping cream to cover everything, she then chose the largest of the chairs in the room and sank heavily into it. Alex steered Annie over to the tea table and supervised her birdlike helpings before he, too, covered his plate in cake and whipped cream. He followed Annie over to the other side of the room and sat in the chair next to hers. Annie looked unhappier than Ruth had ever seen her, and her heart went out to her.

"Oh, my dears," Aunt Florence was now expounding thickly through a mouthful of scone, "you've no idea at your young and carefree ages how it is for such as me. Not, mind you, that I am that far advanced in years." She glanced coyly at Alex. "I do have a grown daughter, I admit, but I married very young. Angus was in a dreadful hurry, and I gave in to him. But now here I am, far before my time, a widow. It is a dreadful thing, a dreadful thing." She reached down into the depths of her quivering bosom and produced a large, lacy hankie with which she dabbed her eyes.

Alex leaped up and offered her his handkerchief as well.

"There, there now, Mrs. Campbell, please don't upset yourself. I'm sure everything will turn out fine. Just remember to have faith in the One above. I once trained for a minister, and I know how much comfort one's religion can give at a time like this."

Florence took his handkerchief and placed it tenderly into her bosom. "Thank you so much, Alex." She looked up tearfully at him. "You must call me Florence. I feel so close to you already."

Ruth had the uncomfortable feeling she was intruding on an intimate family discussion. She looked over at Annie for support. Annie was staring with undisguised disgust at Alex and her mother. Ruth was shocked at the frankness of her expression, but Alex turned around to return to his chair, and Annie's expression was quickly replaced with a smile of polite approval. Ruth wondered if she had imagined Annie's disgust, but Florence had recovered her composure and was already addressing her.

"Alex is not at all like his cousin, Douglas MacPherson, you know, Ruth, my dear. Alex is truly a gentleman. In fact, he has been kind enough to come all the way out here to check up on his cousin, merely out of the goodness of his own heart. It seems that because of his religious convictions, Dr. MacPherson is always getting himself into scrapes of one sort or another. Not that religious convictions are altogether a bad thing, mind you. We all must be true to our religion, but everything in moderation, I say. It just doesn't do to become fanatical about these things."

Ruth, who was the main target of this address, smiled weakly. She wasn't quite sure how to answer, but she needn't have bothered, because Florence was not looking for Ruth's opinion, she was informing her of it. She continued.

"Now, Ruth, I insist that you do not become too chummy with this cousin of Alex's. I know he is concerned for your welfare what with taking your father into the hospital, but after all, it was his fault that your father was hurt in the first place. Don't forget that, Ruth. You really must put a proper distance between yourself and him. I insist upon it!

"By the way," she continued regally, "I will take charge of your father's care from now on, and I will make sure he is properly looked after. I came here to tell you that I went up to Nairobi for a couple of days this week. Your father is not at all well, but it is really no wonder with the nursing care they provide in that hospital. It's a wonder anyone comes out alive! And the hygiene! Appalling!" She sniffed with disgust. "It is far beyond your capabilities to deal with those things. I have instructed that long drink of water, Dr. Burgess, that he be under continual care. I will have nothing but the best for him, my dear, don't you worry about that!"

"Aunt Florence!" Ruth was taken completely by surprise. "You never mentioned that you saw my father! Will he be able to come home soon? What did Dr. Burgess tell you? Is he getting better?" It was humiliating to have to glean any news of her father from Aunt Florence, but Ruth was desperate. She didn't even care that her aunt was taking control of his care.

"Well, as far as I am concerned, he is in terrible hands. He should really be nursed at home, the way I nursed my dear Angus. But one can't really do a thing once those doctors get hold of them. Of course, since he won't have anything to do with you for having put him in there and with the help of that dreadful MacPherson man, Alex, here will keep you abreast of your father's condition for me, so you may feel free to drop Dr. MacPherson altogether. Again, I insist on it." She looked over at Alex and smiled triumphantly.

Ruth felt tears of fury and shame flooding into her eyes. She desperately blinked and swallowed them back. She glanced over at Annie, but Annie just sat and looked helplessly back at her. She looked at Florence. Florence took a sip of her tea and continued, taking Ruth's silence for consent.

"Of course, I have taken all the necessary steps to prevent a native hospital from being established by Dr. MacPherson. Tourism is such an important industry in this town, I would insist that nothing jeopardizes it. Least of all, a hospital that would draw in hundreds of undesirables from all over the country."

Ruth could hardly believe Aunt Florence was talking about this hospital when her father was so ill. But recklessly, she threw out a defense. She just couldn't let Aunt Florence off this particular hook. "But, Aunt Florence, don't you think that it would be good for the hotel to have people coming into Campbellburgh? They will need a place to stay."

Ruth instantly realized her mistake.

"Good heavens! How can you possibly suggest such a thing? To have my hotel filled with riffraff and goodness knows what! I would rather sell it and move to Timbuktu! Ruth, I am surprised at you!" Ruth reached for her hat but, of course, she wasn't wearing it. She clasped her hands in her lap and stared at them nervously. Stupid mistake, she thought to herself.

"Well, Miss Jones," Alex was condescendingly addressing her. She really couldn't stand this man, and she wondered what on earth Douglas tolerated him for. Maybe there was something wrong with Douglas after all. "I really feel it is my duty to warn you not to get too involved with my cousin. I have known him all my life, and while I love him as a dear relative, it is important to keep things in perspective. He is rather fanatical in his beliefs. He has been that way from childhood. He gets it from his mother, God bless her soul, poor woman. If it hadn't been for the good sense of her husband, she would have given away everything she had. People were constantly taking advantage of her generous nature and, unfortunately, she had a great effect on Douglas. Although he has many commendable ideas about helping the disadvantaged and destitute, we must try to keep our good deeds on a reasonable level so that they don't interfere with people who are just trying to make an honest living.

"So, Miss Jones," he concluded, "I suggest you not get yourself involved in something that your family would find most regrettable. And, regrettably, this is a time when they desperately need all you can give them. May I add that you do have my heartfelt prayer for your father's quick and complete recovery." He smiled charmingly, but Ruth was suddenly left with the most unreasonable impression she had been spat at.

Ruth forced herself to sit quietly. She wanted to run away, but if she did anything, she should stand up and defend Douglas. She was frozen with the fear of making another mistake. She felt like a complete coward. She sat in shameful silence.

Milka returned with a fresh pot of tea and some more cake. For a few golden moments, there was silence while they waited for Milka to finish passing the food around.

As Milka left, Florence decided to change the subject to something more pleasant. She turned toward Annie, who sat with Alex at her side. "Of course, we are so fortunate to have the pleasure of Mr. Kendall's company in our town. I have invited him to stay with us during his sojourn in Campbell-burgh, and I feel he has, even in this short time, become the son to me that I never had." She paused and looked significantly at Annie, who blushed and avoided her gaze. Alex Kendall smiled and basked openly in her approval of him.

Florence, pleased with his response, continued, "After all I have been through with the death of my dear husband, it has been a great consolation to me that the good Lord above has at last seen fit to send someone to be a solution to the desperate straights I so unhappily find myself in."

She lapsed into a woeful recounting of her tribulations. "No one knows," she began tearfully, "how hard it is for me these days. I have deeper sorrow than I ever thought I would have in this life. I can't even bring myself to mention the most painful part of it to anyone. The burden is entirely my own." And she broke down into a flurry of sobs. Annie jumped up and rushed over to comfort her mother.

"There, there, Mother, everything will be all right, you'll see. I know it will. You are just rather overwrought with Uncle Jack being ill. Come along, you'll be yourself again soon."

"Yes, perhaps you're right," replied Florence, blowing her nose, "but I do feel a little weak." She stood up and took Annie's arm. "I must go home now. Alex, please come here, my dear." Alex rushed over and took her other arm, and together they led her outside to the waiting surrey. They settled her into her seat with much fuss and bother, while Ruth stood watching the scene incredulously.

Poor, poor, Annie, she thought, *Aunt Florence is scheming to marry her off again.*

"Now, remember, Ruth," Florence launched her parting shot, "you will no longer have anything more to do with Douglas MacPherson. I simply won't have it!" The buggy started with a sudden jerk, and Annie turned over her shoulder and waved sadly to Ruth.

Ruth spent a fitful night thinking about Annie and her new predicament with Alex Kendall. Every now and then she relived the shame and embarrassment of Aunt Florence's attack on her and her relationship with Douglas. And over and over again, she cringed shamefully at the memory of her father's furious face glaring at her in helpless hatred from his hospital bed. Tendrils of bitterness and anger wound themselves around and around her broken heart, binding it painfully together again in an unnatural wholeness.

In the morning Ruth woke with a sense of cold resolve. She would take the milk money out of the cash box and head into town with the milk cart. She would visit Mrs. Singh's and order the most beautiful dress Mrs. Singh could make for her. She didn't care how ugly she was. If Aunt Florence thought she had designs on Douglas MacPherson, let her think the worst! She would never again be without at least one dress in which to receive visitors. And she resolved not to care what her father thought. She didn't regret cutting up that ugly, old tweed skirt.

Later that morning, when she rode angrily into town behind

the milk cart, the milk money burning a hole in her pocket, she noticed that Rosie was parked outside the Campbell Arms Hotel. Impulsively, she turned Chui down the drive, calling to the milk cart driver to go ahead without her.

As she rode into the circular driveway past the large, white Campbell Arms sign, she realized it had been years since she had actually set foot on the grounds. This was the heart and hub of the Campbell empire. This was the source of their money and their power.

She was surprised at how old the place looked now that she was up close. The white paint on the outside of the big main building was worn and dull, and the thatched roof was ragged around the edges and paled by too many years in the glaring heat. Even the gardens looked rather dry and faded. But there was still an air of stately elegance about the old place that was in no way diminished by its slight slip into shabbiness.

There were wide, curved steps leading up to a veranda covered by a massive old bougainvillaea. To the left of the main building were the rondavels, little thatched circular huts where the guests stayed, stretching out in a curved line that circled the lawns. On the right side, the veranda opened out into a wide patio, where tables were set among potted palms and flowering bushes.

Ruth pulled Chui to a halt in front of the steps where Rosie was parked and realized that she had no idea what she was doing here beyond the ever-present hope in her heart to see Douglas MacPherson again. Angry with herself, she kicked Chui harder than she meant to, and Chui gave a surprised whinny of pain before setting off at a trot around the far side of the driveway. Hurrying away, embarrassed at herself, she heard someone shout from behind her.

"Ruth! Miss Jones!"

The thought flashed through her mind that she could get

away quickly by pretending she hadn't heard.

"Ruth!" It was Douglas. Blushing with embarrassment and trying to come up with a reason for her presence here, Ruth pulled Chui to a halt and turned him around slowly.

Douglas was standing on the veranda by the tables waving Ruth over to him. "Hey, Ruth!" She waved back self-consciously. "Come and join me for lunch. You're not doing anything urgent, are you?"

Douglas stood smiling a cheerful welcome at her, looking for all the world as if he were waving to a long-lost friend. She dismounted and tied Chui's reins on the rail of the veranda. She could feel the eyes of the patrons in the restaurant staring curiously at her. Glancing quickly over them, she thought she recognized several townsfolk. Looking shamefully down at her boots and trousers, she slipped up the steps. Douglas was holding out his hand to shake hers.

"It's great to see a friendly face, here. I'm tired of eating alone all the time. Come and join me. Lunch is on me!"

"Oh, no, really I couldn't. I'm not properly dressed, and the milk. . ."

"Oh, nonsense, we've been through all this before!" He steered Ruth to his table and pulled out her chair. Ruth sat down obediently, aware of the eyes of several of the townspeople openly staring at this interesting little rendezvous.

"Waiter, another coffee," called Douglas, "and how about some of that delicious mango salad you were serving this morning?" He turned to Ruth. "I don't know what they do to it, but it's really worth trying." Ruth smiled. She felt ridiculous, but it was worth it to be here just to have him smile at her like that.

"Have you heard from your father? How is he?" Ruth snapped to attention.

"Aunt Florence came to see me yesterday. I couldn't really get a clear answer from her, but I'm afraid he is rather ill." Douglas's face fell.

"Ruth, I am sorry. It is all my fault. Is there anything I can possibly do? I feel simply awful about the whole thing."

"No, no," Ruth protested quickly, shocked to see the remorse on his face. "No, it's not your fault at all. Dr. Burgess told me so himself. In fact, it is a good thing he hurt his leg, otherwise he would never have received the treatment he needs. It's his liver. It's because he. . ." Suddenly she stopped. Douglas was such a good person. She felt embarrassed to explain her father's drinking.

"Have you made any progress with building your hospital?" she asked suddenly, pleased to have thought of a new subject.

Douglas sighed. "I think I have been completely stone-walled here. I'm going to try somewhere else, perhaps all the way into Uganda. It's funny. I was so certain this was the spot for the hospital. I even thought I had God's guidance to find the very place." He shook his head and spoke very quietly, "I guess I must have made a mistake."

"Don't give up just yet," Ruth blurted out. "There must be a way. You said that God wanted the hospital here. He will surely find a way then. You can't give up so easily." Douglas looked up at her in surprise. Ruth was surprised herself. What an outburst, she thought, looking down at her lap. What on earth has come over me these days?

Douglas was speaking. "Thanks for your vote of confidence, Ruth. I appreciate it. But I think you're the only person in this entire town who feels that way. I must have misinterpreted God's leading me here. I was mistaken." He looked defeated and discouraged.

"I'm sure something will come up," she said, still anxious to find him a solution. "Well, surely she can't tie up every place that's for sale in town?"

"Maybe she can. And in any case, she has a lot of influence."

"I'm sorry your cousin Alex has not been able to help you with my aunt," Ruth said, wondering how he fit in.

Douglas sighed deeply again. "It was a terrible mistake for him to come here, worse than you'll ever know. I fear my cousin has designs on Annie. I really must leave Campbellburgh, and I am trying to persuade him to come with me. The trouble is that he is staying with the Campbells. Florence has taken a liking to him, and I can't get him to agree to come with me."

Just then, the concierge of the hotel appeared beside their table. Ruth looked up in surprise. When she saw his face, a chill went down her spine.

"Miss Jones." He leaned over confidentially. "Dr. Burgess from the Nairobi hospital is on the emergency radio. He would like to speak with you." The color drained from her face, and she stood up weakly. Douglas came and took her arm.

"How did he know I was here?"

"He didn't," explained the concierge. "He just called with a message, but I explained you were dining here, so he asked if he might speak to you himself."

"It's all right, Ruth, steady now." Douglas was walking her into the darkness of the lobby. "It may only be a small thing." Ruth was glad for his comforting presence, but she knew people didn't use the emergency radio for small things.

When she heard Dr. Burgess's voice on the radio, the familiar sickness in the pit of her stomach reappeared and began to rise into her throat. "Miss Jones, I am so glad to find you at the hotel." He paused and took a deep breath. "I'm afraid I have very bad news about your father. He suffered a massive heart attack early this morning, and there was nothing we could do to save him. I'm terribly sorry, Miss Jones." Ruth was silent. Her nightmares had come to take over her waking hours.

Douglas reached for the radio. "Stephen, this is Douglas. We'll be in touch with you later. I'll let you know what to do with Mr. Jones. Over and out." He turned to Ruth. "Come along, Ruth, come to my room for a few minutes. Then, I'll drive you home; but first you probably need a couple of minutes of privacy to compose yourself."

Ruth was grateful for his thoughtfulness and his calm control of her situation. She couldn't think. She couldn't even see anything. Tears were smoldering like hot coals in her eyes. She allowed Douglas to take her by the arm and lead her outside. She could smell the damp, sweet riverside scents as they walked along the walkway in front of the hotel. When they came to Douglas's rondavel, he opened the door; and leaving it open, he had Ruth lie down on the bed.

She curled into a ball and started to cry. The loneliness was unbearable, already. No one in the world had ever been alone like she was alone now. She felt that everything and everyone in the world had been wrenched away from her and were now far, far away on the other side of an immense abyss. She was all alone forever and ever.

Douglas sat on the bed next to her with his hand on her shoulder, but he may as well have been on the far side of the moon. After a while, her sobs ran dry and she lay silent. She began to feel grateful for Douglas's touch on her shoulder. It was kind of him, she thought, and the chaos that her life had become suddenly receded a bit.

"If you will be all right for a minute, Ruth, I'll just go and start Rosie and bring her round to pick you up." Ruth didn't move. She wouldn't be all right for a minute and she didn't want him to go, but she couldn't tell him so. He waited for her reply, and when none came, he left. Ruth heard the door close behind him and she started to cry again.

When Douglas came back, she was sobbing deep, agonizing sobs that shook the whole bed.

"Ruth, Ruth!" He rushed over and took her in his arms and hugged her. "Ruth, don't cry so. I know it's a terrible blow, but don't worry, I'll help you out. Whatever you need. Come along now. Wash your face and we'll be on our way. I'll take you home. Milka will be there, won't she?"

Ruth stopped crying and looked up into his face. "It's just that I have no one else left now. He wasn't always the easiest person to live with, but we did have each other. I will miss him terribly."

"I know you will." Douglas took her by the hand and helped her to her feet. He filled the washbasin in the corner for her and she washed her face.

"There, feel a little better now?" He asked with a kind and gentle smile.

"A little." Ruth actually found herself returning his smile.

"Good. Come along now, I'll take you home."

A few minutes later, Ruth found herself speeding along the road to the farm in Rosie. The wind blew into her face, and she let her head fall back against the seat. Letting it blow her sorrow away gave her a temporary respite.

When they arrived at the foothills, Douglas slowed down. Ruth felt strangely exhilarated from the speed, so when Douglas asked her how she was feeling, she was able to smile bravely.

"Tell me," he asked, "how long has your family been farming in up on the hill?"

"My father came here from England forty years ago. He started off by himself, but the Campbells were already settled in the valley, and that's where he met Mother. She died when I was only five." Ruth stopped, and Douglas asked another question.

"Do you think you'll continue to farm the place alone?"

"Yes. Father taught me everything he knew about farming, and I've done it all."

Ruth suddenly had an urge to tell Douglas everything she could about her father and what he had done with his life and what he had done for her. So she talked and talked as they drove the long, winding road up the hill; and Douglas listened and nodded and asked the odd question. By the time they pulled up at the farmhouse, Ruth was actually smiling now and then.

The sound of the approaching motorcar had brought Milka running out onto the veranda to see who it was. Ruth opened the door and ran up the veranda steps to her.

"Oh, Milka," she said. "It's the *bwana*, he's. . .he's. . ." She couldn't get the words out of her mouth before the reality of the pain and the loneliness surged forward again and she started sobbing. Milka rushed forward and put her arms around her.

"Memsahib, '*Sahib*, come inside, come with me." She steered Ruth into the house, whispering comfort from her faith in God. "The Lord will care for you. He comforts those who mourn. He will always be with you. You just let me look after you now." She sat Ruth on a chair and looked over at Douglas, who had followed them inside. "I will get the tea."

Douglas pulled a chair up beside Ruth. "Are you going to be all right alone here tonight? Perhaps I could call on your aunt and she could send someone up to stay with you for the night."

Ruth shook her head, "No thank you, I'll be fine. Really. But I suppose I had better tell my aunt what has happened. She should be the first to know, and Annie, too."

"Don't worry, I'll stop at their place on my way back to town and tell them about your father. Is there anyone else you would like me to tell?" Ruth shook her head again.

"Ruth," Douglas spoke with some hesitation now, "I know you are still overwrought and shocked, but we need to think about making arrangements for the funeral. Would you like me to suggest to your aunt that she help you with that? It may take a load off your mind just now."

The thought of Aunt Florence arranging Father's funeral hit Ruth like a slap in the face. He would never have allowed it if he were alive. "No," she said loudly. "No, not Aunt Florence. I must do it myself. It is the last thing I can do for him. I wasn't even with him when he died. I must at least do this for him. I will speak to the Reverend Montgomery. Father never went to church, but Mother is buried in the churchyard and Father would want to be next to her."

Douglas looked relieved to hear Ruth speak so passionately. Milka brought the tea in and set the tray on the table. She poured Ruth and Douglas each a cup and offered them some scones. Ruth felt she couldn't touch a thing, but Douglas took one gratefully. Milka bustled about making Ruth feel comfortable and making sure she drank her tea.

When Douglas finished his scone, he stood up. "Well, I should go and call on your aunt before it gets too late," he said. "I will also send word to Dr. Burgess to send your father's body down on the train as soon as can be arranged so that we can have the funeral."

"Thank you, Douglas," Ruth said gratefully, using his name for only the second time. "I appreciate everything you are doing. Thank you."

Douglas looked a little embarrassed at her gratitude. "Not at all. I am just glad to be of service. Please let me know at once if there is anything else I can do to help." He looked at Milka. "Look after her tonight."

"Of course I will, *Bwana*. She is like my own child," Milka responded, standing protectively beside Ruth.

"Yes, I know," said Douglas, and then without warning, he leaned down and kissed Ruth on the cheek. "God bless you, Ruth," he whispered in her ear. A moment later he was gone, and Rosie's engine roared and faded away down the road.

seven

The syce from the hotel had brought Chui back that night. In the morning a surrey arrived from Florence with the message that Ruth was to come down to see her now. Ruth sent the surrey back empty, saying that she would call later. She felt too weak to face her aunt just yet. After breakfast, Ruth headed into town. She was numb with the shock of her father's death and she rode absentmindedly.

At the turnoff to the Campbell place, she stopped Chui on the side of the road. She stood looking up the driveway for a long time. She really couldn't face Aunt Florence even yet, so giving Chui a gentle spur, she headed into town. She decided she would make the funeral arrangements, and perhaps she would feel a little stronger once that was behind her; then she would face Aunt Florence.

The whole town already knew of Jack's death. As Ruth rode to the church, several people stopped to offer her their condolences. They spoke to her with quiet respect as they looked up into her tired, unsmiling face. Ruth could tell by their reaction that her grief and loneliness must seem, even to them, like an open wound.

She rode past her mother's land and wondered for a moment what she would do with it now.

Mrs. Montgomery greeted Ruth at her door, and with many kind offers of condolence, she ushered Ruth into her husband's dark, hushed study. The Reverend Montgomery stood up to greet her with an appropriately dignified, yet sorrowful smile on his lips. He offered her a chair in front of his desk.

"I am so glad you have taken the trouble to call on me, my

dear Miss Jones. Mrs. Florence Campbell just left here this morning with the news of your poor father's passing." The Reverend Montgomery offered a bland, polite version of Milka's faith, Ruth thought to herself as she sat stiffly in front of his desk. He explained all the correct protocol of a proper Christian burial, even for such an inveterate sinner as Jack Jones.

"You are so deeply fortunate to have such a fine Christian woman as Mrs. Campbell for your aunt. I'm sure you will derive a great deal of comfort from her presence," he droned. Ruth tried to smile politely and agree. Apparently, he and Aunt Florence had decided that the funeral would be held on the following afternoon. The casket would arrive on tonight's train.

Ruth's polite boredom evaporated with this comment. "Excuse me, Reverend, but I would very much like to make my father's funeral arrangements myself, if you don't mind." She tried to speak firmly, with authority.

"Oh, of course, my dear Miss Jones, of course. But you must be careful not to overdo things in your fragile state, and your Aunt Campbell is so concerned about you. You simply must allow yourself to rely on her help, my dear."

Ruth pulled her chair closer to the reverend's desk and forced herself to go over every detail for the funeral that she could possibly think of. Several times she was interrupted by the reverend. "Miss Jones, please don't let yourself be bothered with such small details. I know that Mrs. Campbell would be most happy to see to such things as the cards and the flowers. I am going to call on her this afternoon, and she has already explained that she is intending to help us."

Ruth sighed and sat back in the chair. In a flat, empty voice she said she would like her father buried next to his wife. The Reverend Montgomery and Aunt Florence had already arranged for that, but the reverend was careful to give Ruth the impression that he agreed to it more for her sainted mother's sake than for her father's.

Ruth was exceedingly irritated at the end of the interview and very glad to get out of the stuffy office into the heat and the sunshine of the African afternoon.

A few minutes later, Ruth climbed the narrow stairs to Mrs. Singh's little shop, which was in a room over her husband's duka. Mrs. Singh warmly welcomed Ruth into her cluttered room. Ruth noticed the large black and gold sewing machine under the single window that looked out over the street. There were long tables and mannequins taking up most of the rest of the room and tape measures, scissors, and pincushions scattered on every available surface. Over in one corner was a mannequin wearing an exquisite white silk wedding gown. Ruth looked at it quickly and thought that it would look lovely on Annie.

Mrs. Singh herself was an elegant woman, wrapped neatly in a yellow sari. The material was delicately interwoven with silver thread, which shimmered as she moved.

"Good morning, Miss Jones," she said, her lilting voice strongly tinged with an Indian accent. "It is my pleasure to see you here. Please accept my deepest condolences on the death of your father. You will no doubt miss him terribly."

"Thank you, I will," mumbled Ruth, still embarrassed at the sorrow that people felt for her loss. But Mrs. Singh floated toward her and led her to a richly brocaded gold armchair, the only chair in the room besides the one at the sewing machine. She motioned for Ruth to sit.

"How may I be of service to you?" She bowed slightly and smiled warmly, pulling her chair away from the sewing machine and sitting opposite Ruth.

"It will be my father's funeral tomorrow," Ruth began, "and I would like to have a new dress for the occasion. Would it be possible to have one readied that quickly?"

Mrs. Singh smiled. "For such an important occasion, I would be happy to be of service to you. It would be helpful, of course, if we could choose a dress with quite a simple pattern. Did you have something particular in mind?"

Ruth felt embarrassed at her lack of knowledge of the intricacies of dressmaking. "No, I don't really know much about dresses," she confessed, "but something simple would suit me, too. And perhaps not in black, either. Maybe a blue," she added impulsively. She couldn't face another black dress like her mother's.

Mrs. Singh stood up and pulled a bolt of fabric from behind a curtain. "With your very beautiful red hair and fair complexion, perhaps this green would be nice. It is quite dark, but lightweight, and would not look too out of place in the church."

She held the fabric out for Ruth to touch. It was silky and had a delicate leaf pattern woven right into the material. Ruth thought she had never seen anything so lovely in her life.

Ruth was still fingering the fabric. She could hardly believe that she could actually wear something so pretty, and to a funeral, too. "It's lovely," she said.

"Let me measure you," said Mrs. Singh, pulling a tape measure that was hanging around her neck. Ruth stood up and Mrs. Singh wrapped the tape around her.

Suddenly Ruth had a worrying thought. "Will it cost very much money?" she asked quickly. "The material, I mean."

"No, no, not too much. I will keep the price down by making your dress very simple. Let's see, we will need about three and a half yards." Mrs. Singh's voice trailed off as she calculated the cost of the dress.

When she finally came up with a figure, Ruth was pleasantly surprised to discover that her milk money more than covered it. As she left, she felt she was ready at last to face

Aunt Florence. She hoped the Reverend Montgomery wouldn't be there.

Juma, the Campbells' houseboy, ushered Ruth into the dark, scented lounge where Florence was sitting drinking tea with Annie and Alex.

"Miss Jones is here, *Memsahib*," Juma announced. Florence stood up and turned around in surprise.

"Oh, my goodness," she declared, "I was expecting the reverend." She descended on Ruth and kissed her brusquely on the cheek. "I am so sorry about your father, my dear child, but just because you are upset must not cause you to forget your manners. I especially sent my best surrey up to fetch you this morning. I had to go into town in the old buggy, you know. I was really quite a sight to be seen driving around in that old thing, and then you never even came. We were expecting you at luncheon!"

"I'm sorry, Aunt, but I wanted to see the Reverend Montgomery about Father's funeral."

"Ruthie, it is so good you are here at last," interjected Annie, who came over to hug Ruth. "How are you? Are you all right? Dr. MacPherson came by yesterday and told us you were doing quite well and that Milka was taking wonderful care of you."

"I'm fine, thanks, Annie," said Ruth. Alex had reached forward to shake Ruth's hand.

"Please accept my sincere sympathy, Miss Jones," he said in his smooth American accent.

"Thank you," mumbled Ruth in reply, while they all took their seats again.

"Juma, bring a teacup for *Memsahib* Jones," commanded Florence before turning on Ruth.

"My dear child, you have no need to be bothering the Reverend Montgomery about the funeral arrangements. I will look after that. After all, what would a child like you know about holding a funeral?" It was not really a question she intended Ruth to answer because she launched straight into the subject that interested her more. "I am absolutely shocked that you would allow that Dr. MacPherson to drive you home again, after I so explicitly warned you against having anything to do with the man!

"On top of that, I could hardly believe my eyes when he marched up here yesterday, as bold as brass, to inform me of a death in my own family! Informed by a perfect stranger about your own brother-in-law's death because my own niece can't be bothered to come herself!" Florence was working herself up into one of her tirades already.

Ruth sat and listened in near disbelief. She had actually assumed that because her father had just died her aunt may have deigned to show her some sympathy. But here she was, listening to her nearest relative ranting over her poor behavior yet again.

"What do you have to say for yourself, young lady?" demanded Aunt Florence for the second time. And in the moment of silence that followed, it occurred to Ruth that she could say whatever she chose. She had nothing to lose anymore. Her father would never know again whether or not she had been polite to her aunt.

"Aunt Florence," she said standing up, "I have had enough of you trying to run my life. In the first place, I have a right at my age to associate with whomever I please, and I please to associate with Dr. MacPherson. I would appreciate it if you would no longer tell me stories of his evil intentions." She glared over at Alex. "He is a friend of mine.

"And secondly, I didn't come to see you this morning because I want to arrange my own father's funeral. You do not need to arrange it for me—I will do it myself, thank you. If you would, please tell the Reverend Montgomery when he comes that I would like the funeral to be the way he and I discussed earlier."

By now, Florence had risen and stretched to her full height, a good six inches below Ruth's. "I will do no such thing," she spluttered, her face turning a dangerous shade of purple. "Now, you listen to me. . ."

For the first time in her life, Ruth lost her temper. She leaned over Florence and glared down into her eyes. "Yes, you will, and I will not listen to you," Ruth hissed slowly through clenched teeth. To her utter astonishment, Florence was taken aback. She sat back in her chair.

"Oh dear," she began in a mournful tone, "I suppose there is nothing I can do. After all I've done for you, you no longer even listen to me. I see, poor woman that I am, I am utterly powerless to prevent you from doing whatever you want.

"I am to see my own brother-in-law buried without even so much as a thank-you-very-much from his daughter for the help I try to give her in her time of need. Then, I am mortified in front of my entire family." She paused and blew her nose.

"Dear, would you fetch me another hankie? This one is completely used up. Oh, dear, what am I to do?" Alex jumped up, and she wailed pitifully. Ruth was transfixed with anger.

How dare she criticize the funeral arrangements she had made for her own father, as if Florence had ever given him more than the time of day when he was alive. Ruth sat simmering with fury, speechless, impotent, and angrier than she had ever been before. The bonds that had kept her tied up and submissive all her life had strained to their breaking point.

The minute Alex was out of earshot, Florence turned on Ruth. The whimpering widow had vanished. "I know all about your Dr. MacPherson," she snarled, "trying to lure sheltered young women into his web of intrigue so that he can use them for his own ends. You aren't the first, and you won't be the last." Alex returned with the handkerchief, and Florence suddenly burst into renewed tears.

"I'm sorry that is your opinion of Dr. MacPherson, Aunt Florence, but it isn't true," said Ruth furiously. "How dare you call yourself a Christian and yet spread evil lies about a fine Christian missionary!"

Florence uttered a pitiful little scream and threw herself onto Alex's shoulder. "Oh, dear, what have I ever done to deserve this?" wailed Florence. Annie and Alex were both hovering over her. Annie was flapping a hankie over her face to give her air. "I am going to be ill. Quickly fetch some smelling salts and some brandy. Oh, lay me down on the couch. Oh, dear, what will become of me, and Angus so recently departed, too. Oh, oh, oh, oh."

Ruth watched the performance in cynical rage, turned heel, and went outside. But as she closed the door behind her, she glanced over her shoulder. Annie was standing up by her mother staring at Ruth in surprise and awe. Ruth smiled. Annie smiled back. The world seemed far away and very calm.

&

As Ruth rode back into town the next morning for her father's funeral, her heart was filled with apprehension for what her aunt would do to repay her for her behavior the day before. But with newfound courage, she no longer gave in to the fear. She wrestled it off. It was hard sometimes, when the fear circled its long cold claws around her chest and nearly squeezed her breath away; but she broke out of its grip time after time and told herself she was no longer afraid of Florence. She could do no more to hurt her.

The big old baobab tree on the way into town stood welcoming her onto the plains like an old friend. The huge boils of wood no longer seemed grotesque to Ruth, but were now the familiar blemishes and scars on the face of one you have loved for a long time. The guinea fowl squawked and scattered, and she smiled as she rode by.

The little church where her father would be buried looked as lonely and empty as Ruth's own future, but Ruth rode right past and went straight into town to Mrs. Singh's shop. She had the money for the dress stuffed into the pocket of her trousers, and she fingered it once more as she tied Chui to the hitching post outside the duka.

Mrs. Singh greeted her with her warm welcoming smile. "Come in, come in, Miss Jones. Your dress is all ready. I just finished hemming it this morning. I think you'll be very pleased, very pleased indeed!"

She floated over to a mannequin standing by the wedding dress that Ruth had noticed the day before, and there was the loveliest dress Ruth had ever seen. A simple bodice with short, capped sleeves and a full skirt with a thin white belt at the waist. Ruth gasped with pleasure.

"Are you sure it will look as nice on me as it does on the mannequin?" asked Ruth shyly.

Mrs. Singh laughed delightedly. "Well, try it on and we'll see!" Carefully, she pulled the dress off and brought it over to Ruth.

One hour later, Ruth walked out of Mr. Singh's duka in her green dress, new silk stockings, and brown boots with buttons up the side. "Oh Chui, I can't possibly ride you to the church in this getup. We'll have to walk," she said, untying the horse. "But we still have lots of time."

Ruth was half embarrassed and half proud of all the attention she attracted as she walked through town. Men politely tipped their hat to her, and women nodded with undisguised curiosity. Being an object of admiration was strange and exhilarating. Ruth nodded back at each one of them until she reached the church. It was early and no one was there yet.

The thought of paying a call on the Montgomerys again sent a shudder down her spine. She walked past the church and out to her mother's land.

As she walked along the side of the dusty road, she heard the roar of a motorcar approaching. It was heading toward town. Ruth stopped, expecting to see Rosie round the curve ahead. But the car that appeared wasn't Rosie. It drew up alongside Ruth, and a man Ruth had never seen before leaned out of the window and pulled a cigarette out of his mouth, blowing the smoke toward Ruth. Another man leaned forward and eyed Ruth lecherously. "Would you be so kind as to tell me where I might find Mr. Kendall?" he asked.

Ruth had an irrational feeling that she shouldn't tell them where to find him. But, she thought, Campbellburgh is a small place, and if I don't tell them where to find him, I don't suppose they will have much trouble finding someone who will. Ruth pointed in the direction of Florence Campbell's house up on the hill behind them. "He stays there," she said. The man put the cigarette back into his mouth, tipped his hat, and turned the car around with a squeal of the tires. Ruth shuddered, glad they were gone, and wondered what Aunt Florence would make of them.

She turned Chui into her mother's land and led him down to the river. On the way down, she stopped to pick flowers from some of the bushes growing nearby. She would lay them on her father's casket. Flowers from her mother's land, picked by her hand for her father's burial. Tears flooded into her eyes. A warm breeze blew along the water across the river and rustled the bushes and reeds nearby. Ruth was glad of it. It cooled her damp face and evaporated her tears. She was glad she had taken the trouble to dress for the occasion, the occasion of saying good-bye to her parents. Now she would be completely alone.

After letting Chui drink from the river, Ruth walked back to the church. Other people were beginning to trickle toward it, Ruth noticed. She tied up Chui and walked back to the stone steps of the church, holding tightly to her bouquet. Only a few people were coming compared with Angus Campbell's funeral.

She nodded to Mr. Cooper, the lawyer that she had sat next to at Angus's funeral. Some of the farmers from the surrounding countryside had ridden in, and Ruth tried shyly to acknowledge them, too. She went up the steps and into the dark, stone building. No one else had gone in yet, but the Reverend Montgomery was inside supervising the lighting of the altar candles. Her father's casket was already placed on a table at the front. Slowly Ruth walked up the aisle, clutching her wild bouquet. She carefully placed the flowers on the coffin and sat down in the front pew behind the discreet sign that announced "reserved for family." Hearing her movement, the Reverend Montgomery turned and nodded to her, but his look was stern and unwelcoming. A pang of fear clutched at Ruth again as she realized that he had been told of her behavior by Aunt Florence. She bowed her head and prayed to Milka's God. "Please help me, God, to be strong enough to be alone," she whispered out loud.

Someone slipped into the pew behind her. She froze but didn't dare to look behind her. A few more people came into the church, but Ruth stared ahead. She focused on the flowers she had placed on the coffin and willed herself to think only of the old, old days, when she and her mother and father were all together.

Suddenly there was a loud rustling at the door of the church and Ruth knew that Florence had arrived. She steeled herself. She could see, even without looking, Florence sailing majestically down the aisle in her black silk funeral dress with her black hat swathed in yards and yards of tulle.

There was a blast of eau de cologne as Florence bore down on Ruth's pew far enough to allow Annie and Alex enough room to sit beside her. She shot Ruth a veiled, but hostile glare, and Ruth glued her eyes to the flowers in front of her.

The Reverend Montgomery had a short funeral, as befitting a non-church-going member of the clan by marriage. He kept it simple, the way Ruth had requested, and in a thankfully short space of time, the casket was carried out to the burial plot. Ruth stood up, but Aunt Florence pointedly refused to allow her room, with Annie and Alex escorting her to follow directly behind the casket. Ruth stood to walk behind Florence, humiliated yet again at being outmaneuvered. Annie looked over her shoulder; she had been crying and smiled tearfully at Ruth. It was too much for Ruth. She put her hands to her face and tried to stop her tears. How could I have forgotten to bring a handkerchief to a funeral!

Suddenly an arm went around her waist, and a large man's handkerchief was offered. She looked up into the familiar blue eyes of Douglas MacPherson, who had slipped out of the pew behind her just in time to escort her out to the churchyard. Ruth leaned gratefully against him.

"It's all right, Ruth, come along," whispered Douglas, who had noticed Ruth's dismay. "Just concentrate on saying good-bye to your father. It is for him that we are here, not for them." Then he slipped away quickly before Florence saw him.

Ruth looked straight ahead. The coffin was already in place, and the Reverend Montgomery spoke a few words of comfort to Florence as she approached.

After they had laid Jack to rest, Florence came up to Ruth. She knew Florence wasn't finished with her yet.

"I felt I should come today out of respect for your father, the husband of my dear husband's sister." Florence tossed the words out like a fighter throwing punches to begin the round.

"Although I will tell you that I have never in all my life been treated so rudely as yesterday. And just because you are upset about your father's death is no excuse for such unconscionable behavior." Ruth opened her mouth to protest, but Florence cut her off, "Don't even try to apologize to me, young lady."

Ruth responded in honest surprise, "But, I didn't intend to apologize. And I didn't say those things because I was upset about my father. I said them because I was upset about you."

Florence opened her eyes wide and turned purple. "Well!" she exploded. "Let me tell you, young lady, I know what you are up to, looking like the cat who just ate the cream, even at her own father's funeral. I tell you I am utterly appalled, and the only thing I can be thankful for is that Jack and your dear mother are not here to see it. They are both likely turning over in their graves at this very moment."

Ruth felt this was a rather macabre comment, considering how newly buried her father was and that they were still standing in the cemetery.

"I will thank you not to comment on my parents' attitudes, Aunt Florence," Ruth announced icily, surprising even herself at her boldness.

"Good heavens!" Florence turned to Alex. "Take me home. This is all too much for a poor woman who has just lost her own husband, to be treated this way by someone who I have tried so hard to be charitable to for so many years. And this is all the thanks I get!" Alex handed her a handkerchief as if on cue and led her away.

Ruth turned her attention to Annie, who was coming forward to give her a hug. "I am so sorry about Uncle Jack, Ruth," Annie said. Ruth was surprised to see her looking so shaken. She hadn't even seemed as upset at her own father's funeral, Ruth thought. Annie began to cry as she hugged Ruth, then she whispered quickly. "Mother wants me to marry Alex, and Alex has agreed to marry me, and she says if I don't she will cut me out of her will and disown me. She says it is my duty to marry well. I owe it to her. She has spent all her money on trying to cure father. She can do nothing else now, and she says it is my duty to look after her by marrying Alex."

Ruth listened in horror. She held tight to Annie for a moment. This was ghastly. She had no idea Florence would go to such desperate extremes. Poor, poor Annie.

"In order to prevent me running off, I have to marry Alex on Saturday. This Saturday! Ruth, tell Jimmy for me. And please help me. I have no one else to turn to," she whispered desperately, letting Ruth go.

Florence had, with Alex's obsequious help, recovered her composure. "Let's go, Annie, that's enough!" she bellowed from her surrey.

Ruth sighed and turned toward Chui, who was waiting patiently by the church for her. It was time to start the rest of her life now. She wondered how long she would be able to cope with the loneliness before it drove her mad. But before she had untied Chui, Douglas drove up.

"Come, Ruth, I'll drive you home. You must be very tired."

Ruth thanked him gratefully.

They took Chui to the hotel stables, and then Ruth found herself bouncing along the plains in Rosie yet again. But this time, she felt that she was being led to prison, to a lifetime of solitary confinement. The key had already been thrown away.

She looked down at her hands, conspicuously red and rough against the beautiful green dress she was wearing. But she was still glad she had bought it. It was just a small act of rebellion, and nothing would change; but she wouldn't have missed walking proudly through town this afternoon for all the gold in Sheba. She wondered how much money her father had left her to work with. Even if it was nothing, she was glad she had bought the dress. She put her face into her hands and cried quietly.

The sun was setting behind them as Ruth and Douglas drove into the hills. Golden light flowed like a river from the sun, pouring itself out into the earth until it sank down into the darkness below the horizon. Ruth could feel Rosie's engine pulling against the steep hill. Douglas said nothing, but let Ruth cry quietly as he drove up into the green-gold jewel valley where the brook babbled alongside the road. She was grateful for the silence.

When she looked up at last, they were climbing out of the valley away from the brook. She looked for the spot where the little path that led down to her secret pool joined the road. She remembered the mother and the baby elephant she had seen there; it seemed like eons ago now. All that was left of the joy she had felt watching them play together was only a faded, half-remembered dream.

"Stop. Please," she announced suddenly. She surprised even herself. Douglas looked at her quizzically and brought Rosie to a halt. For a moment there was only the gentle purr of Rosie's engine at rest.

"Come, I want to see something before I go home," said Ruth, pushing the door open beside her. She realized she still had her new dress on, and she paused, wondering if she should just get back into the car. But the thought of driving up to the lonely house with all those dead animals staring down at her from the walls sent a shudder up her spine. Douglas was standing beside Rosie, waiting to see what she would do next. Ruth walked over to the tiny slit in the bush by the road and carefully picked her way past the branches so she wouldn't tear her dress along the path down to the pool where she had seen the elephant. Douglas followed her.

"Where on earth are you going?" he asked, peering through the branches into the little ravine.

Ruth turned to look at him. "Come with me," she said. "There's a pool down here I want to see before we go home." She went slowly and carefully down the little trail, clutching her dress to her legs. The bubbling of the little stream got louder, and the air became cool and dark as they descended. Already the frogs were croaking and the birds were becoming quieter as night fell.

Ruth stepped into the little glade beside the pool. The big thorn tree she had climbed to escape the elephant loomed mysteriously out of the shadows on the far side. Douglas stepped out of the bush beside her.

"Oh, this is beautiful," he whispered, trying not to disturb the peaceful scene before them.

"Yes," Ruth breathed a quiet reply. "I just wanted to come here before I went back to the house." She paused, then added, almost under her breath, "I don't think I can face the loneliness just yet."

"You know," whispered Douglas, "that Jesus can take care of that for you—the loneliness, I mean."

"I don't think He cares too much for me; look what has happened to my life!" Ruth spoke in a normal tone of voice, shattering the peace and beauty of the moment.

"Have you asked Him to care for you?" Douglas responded in a matter of fact tone, as though it was like going to the doctor and asking him to take care of your bunions.

"Oh, Milka does that all the time, but I haven't noticed that it has made any difference to my life."

"But you have to ask Him yourself!" Douglas said. "He won't just waltz in and take over your life because someone else asks Him. He wants your consent. It's you He wants to deal with, not Milka."

Ruth was silent. She had never thought of it that way

before. Had He really not helped her simply because she hadn't asked Him to? The peacefulness of the darkening night quietly crept back into the clearing again. Ruth remembered the elephants, and she felt that perhaps God had been trying to tell her to talk to Jesus then, too. The presence of God reached inside her and touched her. She felt His voice in her mind, immense and loving.

I am here now, Ruth, will you love Me?

No, came Ruth's answer in her heart. *I'm not ready yet.* She still wanted something she could touch and see. She couldn't trust that Jesus would actually stay with her through the long lonely days and years ahead. Ruth looked over at Douglas standing solid and sure beside her.

I love him.

There was silence.

After a little while, Douglas spoke to her of Jesus and what He had done by dying for her on the cross and how He rose again and how it was He who had come to find Ruth and come to live with her. He told her of the Bible and the Church, His own body.

The night was warm and vibrant with life now. Stars thronged across the sky like the numberless herds of game that roamed the plains below. *Cicadas* thrummed relentlessly, beating out their own rhythm and making the very air seem alive with sound. Ruth looked up into the great African night, immense and free, the antithesis of her own heart. She listened to Douglas carefully, but she didn't tell him what she had already told God.

"I will think it all through," she said quietly when he had finished.

"I will pray for you, then," he replied, and they stood together in the night for a few moments.

Finally, Douglas said, "Are you ready to go home now?"

"Yes," Ruth replied. The moon had begun to appear behind

the branches of the thorn tree across the pond. By its light, Ruth could see Douglas looking down at her. He has an odd expression on his face, she thought.

"Ruth, you are beautiful tonight. Your dress shines in the moonlight like your eyes."

Ruth felt her heart skip a beat, and quickly she looked down to hide her thoughts from Douglas. But he stepped toward her and lifted her chin gently up to his face. He bent down and kissed her lips. She closed her eyes and thought she would melt with the warmth that spread all over her body. But as soon as it began, it was over. He took her by the hand and led her back up the dark path. Afterwards Ruth didn't remember anything about how she got home.

The next thing she knew, he was coming around to open the car door for her. They had driven to the house in silence. Ruth could see the lights flickering inside the windows. Milka was waiting for her.

"Thank you for bringing me home, Douglas," she said, getting out of the car.

"Ruth, I'm sorry about what I did at the pool just now. I shouldn't have."

"Don't mention it," mumbled Ruth, turning to run up the steps, but he caught her hand.

"Ruth, wait. I just want to say, I have to leave. I am going to look at some land in Uganda tomorrow. I didn't mean to give you another impression, only you just looked so lovely. I'm sorry, Ruth."

Ruth snatched her arm away from him and ran inside. She ran straight to her bedroom and wept. She wept for her broken heart. She remembered Annie this afternoon, and she wept for Annie's broken heart, too. Milka came in with a cup of tea and tried to comfort her, but she wept until finally she fell asleep, still in her green dress and silk stockings.

eight

It was almost noon when Ruth awoke the next day. She lay in bed and relived the day before. Over and over she thought about Annie and she thought about Douglas, and she remembered how his kiss felt on her lips. After a long time, she got up and wandered into the kitchen. Milka had some meat pies warming in the oven and the kettle simmering on the stove.

"Ah, Memsahib!" she jumped up and rushed over to Ruth. "How are you this afternoon, *'Sabu?*"

Ruth sat down heavily on the kitchen chair and put her head in her hands. "Oh, Milka," she groaned, "I don't think I'll ever be all right again."

" *'Sabu, 'Sabu,* of course you will. It takes time to heal, you know. I pray for you all the time and the Lord Jesus, He will comfort you."

"Oh, Milka, I wish with all my heart that I could believe you, but there is so much wrong, and it is not just because Father is gone now. It is Annie and Aunt Florence, and I don't know what can possibly be done now."

Milka put a meat pie and a cup of tea in front of Ruth and sat down across the table. "Come, come, *'Sabu,* you tell me what the matter is and we will see what can be done."

Ruth talked and ate and drank her tea, and she told Milka all that had happened at the funeral and afterwards. She told Milka about Annie and Jimmy and Alex, and about Douglas, everything she could think of except the little detour they took down to the pool before they came home. Milka listened and nodded sympathetically.

"Well," said Ruth firmly at last when she was finished, "we have to do something for Annie." She felt better for having told Milka everything—almost everything. "All Annie needs is a way to get out of her house and away with Jimmy, just long enough to get married. Once they are married, Florence can do her worst." She thought for a moment. "The first thing we have to do is to tell Jimmy, and we must do it soon. Today is Tuesday and Annie is to be married on Saturday. Tomorrow I should go into town and see Mr. Cooper about Father's estate. First I'll stop at Jimmy MacRae's and tell him what is happening to Annie." Ruth was glad to have something to fill her mind. She could avoid thinking of the years that lay ahead for her, at least for a little while.

❧

When she reached Jimmy's place the next morning, he had seen her coming and was outside waiting to greet her.

"Good morning, Ruth. You're here bright and early. I heard about your father and I am very sorry."

"Thank you," she responded, and dispensing with the preliminaries, she got straight to the point. "Jimmy, I have some more bad news about Annie. We need to talk."

Jimmy's face fell. "Come in. We'll talk inside." He motioned to a chair. Ruth sat down and looked into his anxious face. Her heart went out to him.

"Jimmy, I'm sorry, Florence Campbell really has outdone herself this time. But if we act quickly, we still have time to stop it. She intends to marry Annie off to Alex Kendall this Saturday."

"Good Lord have mercy!" Jimmy leapt up out of his chair and began pacing around the room in desperation. "Surely Annie couldn't have consented to such a plan." Suddenly the color drained from his face, and he sank back down into his chair like a shot antelope. "She hasn't consented, has she?" His voice was small and scared. "Perhaps she has fallen in love with Alex Kendall. After all, he probably has a lot more to offer her than I ever will. I wouldn't blame her."

"Good gracious, Jimmy," exclaimed Ruth. "How could you have so little faith in her? She wanted me to tell you so that you could come and fetch her. She loves you, and she asked me to come to you to tell you to help her. She is desperate. I am really worried about her."

"But, surely, she won't disobey her mother. She clearly told me that she would never do that."

"Jimmy!" Ruth was becoming impatient. "Jimmy, she can't marry a man she doesn't love just to obey her mother. It wouldn't be right. Her mother can't possibly expect her to be unhappily married for the rest of her life. And what about Alex Kendall? It wouldn't be fair to him, either!"

"Well, what can I possibly do to help her?" he asked in his small, confused voice.

Ruth was surprised by her own strength. "Jimmy, we must get word to her that she should leave her house, perhaps in the night. You will meet her and marry her as quickly as you can, then Florence won't be able to do anything about it. Of course, Annie is being watched like a hawk, so it won't be easy. But the important thing, once we get Annie, is to get you two married as soon as possible. Do you know anyone who would be able to do it for you? The Reverend Montgomery would be hopeless. He would never dare do anything to upset Aunt Florence."

"I know a priest up at the French mission. He would probably do it if I asked. But he would have to come over the hills from away out beyond your place. I could send word to him. But how on earth would we be able to get Annie out? Florence has that place guarded like the crown jewels."

The two of them sat in silence pondering their dilemma. Ruth finally spoke up. "If we could get Annie as far as my place, you could meet the priest there and he could marry you. Annie might be able to find a way to slip out just before dawn, while everyone is still sleeping. You could meet her on the road and bring her up to the farm. Florence would likely expect you to run off to Nairobi, so she would probably look there first. Maybe you could go to Uganda? Perhaps you could even throw Aunt Florence off your trail by buying train tickets for you and Annie to Nairobi, even though you don't intend to use them."

Jimmy let Ruth's plan sink in for a few minutes. "How can we let Annie know which night to meet me?"

"Yes, that will be rather a problem, I'm afraid. I've burnt my bridges with Aunt Florence, I fear," answered Ruth. Jimmy sat with his head in his hands. He looked as though he were praying. Ruth sighed. That would be a difficult problem. But all at once she remembered the wedding dress in Mrs. Singh's shop. "That's it!" she burst out. "It is Annie's wedding dress!"

Jimmy nearly jumped out of his skin at Ruth's outburst. "What are you talking about?"

"I was at Mrs. Singh's dressmaking shop," said Ruth excitedly. "She had a wedding dress there. I'm sure it must be for Annie! Who else would be getting married? Annie will be having her fittings there. Mrs. Singh would pass a message to Annie for us! I'm sure she would!"

"Well, I can go and ask her."

"I'll do that for you, Jimmy," laughed Ruth. "I can't imagine Mrs. Singh giving you the details of Annie's dress fittings."

"Thanks, Ruth."

"Don't mention it. You have enough to do anyway. Now, just let me know which night your priest will be coming, and I'll get the message to Annie."

Ruth got up and headed for the door. "Well, Jimmy, all the

best of luck to you." She put out her hand, and he shook it gratefully.

"Thanks, Ruth, you've been a real friend to us both." She flashed him a quick smile and stepped out into the hot midday sun. Pulling her hat low, she rode back into town.

She walked quickly up to Mrs. Singh's shop. Mrs. Singh greeted her with her usual friendly smile. "Come in, come in, Miss Jones. What can I do for you today?"

"Well, I actually only came to ask you a question, Mrs. Singh."

"That is fine, my dear, what question do you have?"

"It is a rather delicate matter," began Ruth, "and it has to do with my friend Annie Campbell. I believe she is to be married shortly, and I wondered if you were making the dress for her."

"Yes, yes." Mrs. Singh smiled broadly. "I have the honor of doing so. It is a rather rushed job, though, so I have been working on it day and night. But it will be very beautiful. Pure white silk with embroidered pearls." She ran over to the mannequin and fetched the dress for Ruth to see.

"It is lovely," smiled Ruth. "Could you tell me if Annie is coming in for a fitting before it is finished?"

"Oh, but of course! I must make certain everything is just so. I am expecting her here tomorrow afternoon."

"Does she always come with her mother?"

Mrs. Singh was becoming a little puzzled at Ruth's line of questioning and rather cautiously affirmed that she did.

"You see," Ruth said because she felt she owed her some explanation, "Annie is not marrying of her own free will. Her mother is keeping all messages from reaching her from her friends. As a result, I wonder if you might give her a message from me and do it without her mother seeing it."

Mrs. Singh's eyes lit up, and Ruth knew she had found herself a coconspirator. "Ah, I wondered why everything was to be so rushed, and with poor Mr. Campbell so recently passed away, too. Poor Miss Campbell, I thought she looked rather distraught. I like her very much and would be most happy to pass a message on from you."

"Thank you, Mrs. Singh. I am very grateful to you, and I know Annie will be, too, and so will the man she wants to marry, Jimmy MacRae."

"Ah, yes, I know him."

"Mrs. Singh, either Jimmy or I will return tonight or tomorrow morning with a message for Annie. Please make sure Mrs. Campbell doesn't see it."

"You can trust me, Miss Jones. I will give it to her inside my fitting room while her mother is waiting outside for her to change. It will be very simple." She bowed slightly and showed Ruth to the door. "Good-bye, Miss Jones, and good luck!"

Ruth went down the narrow stairs and stepped onto the walkway next to the street.

She walked across the street to the little door with Mr. Cooper's sign on it and went shyly in. Her father had dealt with Mr. Cooper from the time when her mother had died. He was a large, methodical, but pleasantly fatherly man, as she remembered. And it was at least an hour later when she came out, her head crammed to the hilt with legal terminology and spinning with new information. Ruth stood outside Mr. Cooper's, blinking into the afternoon sunshine for a few minutes, assimilating the information and adjusting to the glare of the day.

Her mother had been given land in Campbellburgh when she was a child, as all the Campbell progeny had, and her piece consisted of the entire undeveloped plot next to the river. It was a huge piece, much larger than what Jack had led Ruth to believe, and now that Campbellburgh was a growing concern, it was quite a valuable piece of property.

However, as Mr. Cooper so carefully pointed out to her, if Ruth sold the property, the Campbells all had first refusal rights. In reality that meant Florence, as the other Campbells had not flourished to nearly the same extent as Angus had. Most of the rest were simply poor cousins like she was. Her father had left some money in the bank. Not a lot, as Ruth had suspected, but enough for her to continue to run the farm.

She went back to Jimmy's farm to tell him that Mrs. Singh would pass his message to Annie. Jimmy had a look of grim determination on his face when she got there. He had sent a message to his friend at the French mission and expected an answer back tonight. He was counting on Friday night, which was two nights away, to elope. Since the mission was up in the hills beyond the Jones farm, he and Ruth decided that they would all meet at her farm, where the wedding ceremony would take place. If they bought tickets for the train to Nairobi, Florence would most likely search for them there, which would give them some breathing room to escape. Ruth and Jimmy parted company, but not before Jimmy clasped her hand and looked hard at her.

"You're a good friend, Ruth. A real Godsend." Ruth impulsively put her arms around him and gave him a quick hug.

"Good luck, Jimmy. I'll expect you and Annie before dawn on Saturday, unless I hear otherwise." She mounted Chui and shook the reins.

Before going home, she stopped at the pool again. The little valley was as cool and green and refreshing as it always was. Ruth, as always, felt the weight of the world lift off her shoulders as she descended into it. The little river sparkled easily over the mossy rocks and plunged fearlessly into the deep dark pools. Ruth found her grassy glade and pulled off her boots and her hat. She slipped her bare feet into the silky water and leaned back against the smooth trunk of the old tree. It seemed so different in the daytime than at night. She thought about Douglas's kiss. Remembering it made her glad she was doing something to help Annie and Jimmy find the joy and happiness they so deserved.

And she remembered the elephant and its child that were here that time and how she had ached with longing for a life of her own. Everything had changed so much since that day. Soon Annie and Jimmy would be gone, and Douglas was already gone. Her father was gone, and, as far as she was concerned, so was Aunt Florence. The elephants had come and gone. And she was still here, still farming, and still alone. Only now it felt more lonely and painful than it ever had before.

As she sat in the quietness, Ruth made a plan. It was a bold and unusual one, but it was her only hope. She would try it. She herself would ask Jesus to help her to carry it out. She would speak to Him and tell Him of her plan. She would pray for success and leave the results up to Him. If He chose to give her success, then she would know He had listened to her, but if her plan failed. . . She didn't want to face it until the time came, if it came.

She would write Douglas a letter as soon as she found out where to send it. There was very little time left, so she had to act quickly. Otherwise time would slip away from her as inevitably as the water slipped away down the hill. She had no second chance. Ruth reached down and scooped a handful of water onto her face, letting it soak her hair and shirt, and she prayed with all her heart for God to give her success. And when she stood up to put on her boots, she was fixed on her course as steadfastly and surely as the rivers run down to the sea.

nine

At last it was Friday. Ruth spent a long night in her room waiting for morning. She prayed for Annie and wished she could be with her to help her and to comfort her. Poor, poor Annie. What a terrible price to pay for happiness. Ruth looked outside. The stars twinkled peacefully in the infinite night sky as if this were only a night like any other since time began. The insects clicked and chirped into the scented night air as they had done every night since creation. This night was no different. Far away Ruth caught the distant laugh of a hyena, and a cold shiver of fear ran down her spine. She listened for the trumpet of the elephant. The ancient and echoing sound would comfort her, and surely then she would know that everything would be fine in the morning. But there was nothing. The night stretched out interminably into the deep, dark distance.

The minutes, by sheer determination, at last became hours; and the hours inched ever so uncooperatively by until at last most of the night was done. Milka brought in the morning tea long before dawn. Only the faintest shade of gray was discernable on the hills. Ruth dressed in her new green satin dress. The priest had said he would come at six.

And when at last six grudgingly arrived, she went out onto the veranda to look for him. There he was, striding across the eastern meadow, in the slanting morning sun, as though he had only just been created out of the earth itself.

Ruth was surprised at how young he was. He must only be in his midtwenties, she thought, and with his fair hair and fair skin, the long cossack he wore was oddly incongruous.

But his eyes were alive with the conviction of his faith, and when Ruth reached out to shake his hand, he grasped it firmly and warmly. He spoke with a heavy French accent.

"*Bonjour,* Miss Jones. I am Brother Jean. My friend Jimmy MacRae has spoken very well of you. It is very kind of you to assist him like this."

"I am glad that you were able to come," said Ruth, ushering him into the lounge. The curtains were open and the morning light poured inside like liquid gold, reflecting on the dark wooden floor and the dark tables.

He had walked a long way from the mission in the hills, and he was hungry. They had breakfast together in the dining room. Milka bustled about enthusiastically. She considered it a great honor to serve such a man of God. Ruth, however, had no appetite.

"How do you know Jimmy MacRae?" Ruth asked, making conversation, a new skill she was learning.

"He came to our Christmas Eve mass two or three years ago. We have a very beautiful service. It is truly a time of worship. Jimmy and I got talking and we have remained friends ever since. He regularly comes to the mission to worship with us. He is a fine man. Your friend will be fortunate, indeed, to have him for a husband."

"Yes, I know. I only hope that Annie was able to escape last night. I am so worried."

"Yes, it is a very unfortunate situation. Mrs. Florence Campbell is well known in our area for her views on native education and hospitals. I think she is indeed a very difficult woman. Her daughter has my deepest sympathy. We French, you know, even in the priesthood, never like to stand in the way of true love." He smiled warmly and continued, "But I do not think Jesus stands in the way of true love, either, so I have prayed for Jimmy and Annie, and I am sure the Lord will hold them in the palm of His hand."

Ruth liked this man. She decided to risk her idea of having the wedding in the little valley.

"Since it will be such a rushed wedding for Annie," she began tentatively, "I thought that I might try to make it a little bit special for her. There is a little river valley on the farm, and in the valley is one of the most beautiful spots I have ever seen. The road from town, the one on which Annie and Jimmy will arrive this morning, goes very close to it. I wondered if it might not be a rather lovely spot to hold the ceremony." Ruth felt a little insecure suggesting such an unusual location. She was relieved when she saw him smile with delight at the thought of it.

"Why, yes, I think that would be most romantic to have an outdoor wedding. After all, there is nothing to make the day beautiful but God's own creation. It is a lovely idea."

"I hoped you would agree," said Ruth. "If we start to walk there, we could intercept Annie and Jimmy on the road, and I could take you all to the spot."

As soon as Brother Jean was finished eating, they set off. The dew was thick and wet on the dust of the road, so they left dry footprints and lifted thick clods of mud up with their shoes. Brother Jean carried his Bible and looked refreshed and filled with cheerful anticipation. Ruth, on the other hand, was a bundle of jagged nerves. She wished she could know if Annie was safely in Jimmy's buggy, wending her way up the hillside.

As the road slipped into the little ravine, they thought they could just make out the sound of an engine rising from the valley below. And within a few minutes, they saw Rosie roaring up the road toward them. Annie was in the front seat and saw them first.

"Ruthie," she shrieked, waving wildly. Ruth waved back and ran down the road to meet her. In her excitement, it didn't occur to Ruth that she wasn't expecting them to come with

Douglas. Annie jumped out of the car and threw her arms around Ruth. "Oh Ruth, I am so glad to see you. Jimmy told me what you did. Thank you! Thank you from the bottom of my heart!"

"Annie, I'm so glad to see you. I haven't slept a wink all night worrying about you. How did everything go? Did you get out without being detected? It must have been a dreadful ordeal!"

Annie laughed, "I'd like to say it was and that I was very daring and brave, but all I did was walk out of the house. Mother will be beside herself with fury when she discovers I've gone. I was shaking in my shoes as I left, but not one of the dogs barked at me. In fact, they followed me all the way down the road, and I sent them back just before I met Jimmy and Douglas."

"Douglas?" Ruth looked up, and sure enough there standing by the door of the car stood Douglas. He was watching her.

"Hello, Ruth, how are you doing?" He put out his hand and shook hers warmly. Ruth suddenly felt overwhelmed with shyness, and she could hardly raise her eyes to meet his. He was still looking down at her. "You look beautiful in green, especially in the morning light like this." He spoke almost longingly, but suddenly catching hold of himself, he said more loudly, "I returned for what I thought was Alex's wedding, but instead Jimmy asked me to come out and stand up for him." But Ruth was looking down. She had never heard a longing note in his voice before, and she was too shy to let him see how it made her feel.

"I'm going to drive them to Uganda tonight," he went on. Ruth wondered if she had been given a chance to carry out the plan she had devised. Would she have the courage?

"Oh, I'm so glad," she managed to say. "That will be so much safer for them."

Jimmy and Brother Jean were talking together. Brother Jean had told Jimmy about Ruth's idea for a wedding down by the river and Jimmy was pleased.

"Come along, I'll show it to you," Ruth said. They all got into the car.

When they reached the little path, Ruth led the way down. The sunshine came slanting in horizontally through the leaves, which were aflutter with birds who burst into the most joyful repertoire of music she could imagine for a wedding. The pool shone like a mirror, doubling the beauty of the trees above it. The stream whispered its way over the rocks as though it was in awe of the beauty of the new day.

"Oh, Ruthie, this is the perfect place," whispered Annie.

"It is indeed," agreed Jimmy quietly. They stepped over the stones to cross the river.

"Well," Brother Jean spoke when they were all across, "I suppose we shall begin." He stood under the canopy of an acacia tree, the grass spread out at his feet like a carpet.

"Just hold on a minute!" Douglas had stepped out of sight in the undergrowth just beyond the stream. "I'm just fetching something for the bride."

Annie laughed nervously, and Jimmy reached out to hold her hand. Ruth watched them standing together in her special place, which would now be forever theirs. They looked so beautiful, with the golden sun making a bridal wreath of light on Annie's blond hair. Her simple, soft yellow dress was a perfect color for the green bower that would be her wedding chapel. Jimmy was looking at her as though he would burst with pride.

"Here we are!" Douglas burst out of the bush, his arms full of flowers. "You can't have a wedding without flowers for the bride." He held out a cascade of red and yellow forest flowers that Ruth had seen a thousand times in the bushes and trees. They made a beautiful bouquet. Annie carefully picked a yellow and white frangipani flower out of the bouquet and put it in her hair. Douglas was right; now she looked like a real bride.

"There," he said, "that's better!" And he turned to Ruth and gave her another bouquet. Ruth took it and looked up to thank him. As he smiled down at her, her heart missed a beat. Surely there was more to his look than his usual kindness. How could she know for certain? And yet it seemed to Ruth that the sun shone more brilliantly through the leaves and her flowers exuded a deeper, more passionate scent than they had the moment before. Annie's smile was even more joyful than she could have imagined it ever would be. She went over to Annie. Douglas was sticking a huge bird of paradise flower in Jimmy's buttonhole. She drew Annie away from them.

"Come, Annie, you must have an aisle to walk down." They went to the far end of the clearing and waited for Douglas to organize the men. Ruth whispered, "If you listen to the music of the river and the birds, it will be the loveliest wedding march ever heard—God's own music."

"I know it will be, Ruthie. I can't believe I'm going to be married." She looked at Ruth, suddenly panic stricken. "Even after all that I've been through, I'm terrified."

Ruth suddenly felt the same way. "You know," she answered solemnly, "I would be, too, if I were getting married."

Annie laughed nervously. "Thanks very much, Ruthie. You certainly know how to make someone feel better!" Ruth laughed, too.

"Come along, you two!" Douglas called. "This is no time to start giggling. We have a wedding to attend. Let's go!"

The men were arranged in a row under the tree. Brother Jean had his Bible open, and Jimmy and Douglas were standing at attention to the side. Ruth and Annie looked at each other, and Ruth gave Annie a quick hug. "God bless you, Annie," she said, and like a bridesmaid, Ruth turned and walked slowly toward Jimmy and Douglas. She could see Jimmy proudly watching Annie behind her.

As she reached the front, she caught Douglas's eye. He smiled at her, and it was as though they were alone. The birds were singing for them and the sun was shining on only the two of them. And Ruth knew what she must do.

Annie was next to her now, and Brother Jean began the wedding. As Annie and Jimmy repeated their vows to each other, Ruth's eyes filled with tears. She always thought people who cried at weddings were a little soft in the head, yet here she was doing it herself. But her heart was truly moved to see two such fine people standing here before God, promising to love each other for the rest of their lives. It was the first time she had ever understood how much that meant, and her heart overflowed with joy for them.

When Jimmy had kissed his bride and they were well and truly married, the five of them stood in the little glade in silence. It was as though Jesus Himself were pronouncing a benediction for them. A breath of wind passed through the trees above them and as it went, it parted the leaves and a shaft of sunlight shone down on them. A moment later it was gone and everything was still.

"May I be the first to wish you all of God's blessings on your marriage." Douglas spoke while he reached out to shake Jimmy's hand and leaned forward to kiss the bride.

"Oh, Annie, I'm so happy for you both. God bless you." Ruth hugged Annie and kissed Jimmy.

❧

Back at the house, Milka had set out a brunch on the veranda. She had taken out Ruth's mother's best linen and crystal. There were vases of flowers and bowls of fruit. Ruth gasped. She hadn't seen the linen since she was a very little girl, and the crystal had only sat quietly in the cupboard year in and year out. Milka was standing shyly to the side, smiling with pleasure.

"I hope you don't mind me using your mother's things, *'Sabu* Ruth, but I thought that Miss Annie deserved the very best for her wedding."

"Milka, thank you. You have outdone yourself this time."

"Milka, you shouldn't have!" Annie added.

" *'Sabu* Annie, may I congratulate you on your marriage. May it be filled with God's blessings and be fruitful and long. And congratulations to you, too, *Bwana*." She spoke to Jimmy and beamed with pleasure. Then she turned to Douglas. "Welcome again, *Daktari* MacPherson." She turned and smiled slyly at Ruth before leaving to fetch the first course.

After the meal, Brother Jean took his leave and headed back through the hills. The four of them stood on the veranda watching Brother Jean disappear across the fields.

Jimmy turned to his bride. "Would you like to accompany me for a walk?" Annie smiled up at him. Jimmy looked at Douglas. "It's going to be a long drive to Uganda, and Annie and I haven't had a chance to talk for so long. A few minutes' delay won't hurt anything, will it?"

Douglas smiled at the newlyweds. "We should leave here in an hour." Jimmy took Annie's hand, and they started off down the hill, back to the valley.

Ruth watched them go. Jimmy had put his arm around Annie's shoulders and she leaned her head on his. *They are made for each other,* Ruth thought. *They have a lifetime of joy. No matter what happens, they will be together to love and help each other.* And watching them, she felt immensely alone. The loneliness reached around her like the touch of ice-cold fingers. She felt herself grow breathless in fear. One hour and she would be all alone. All alone forever and ever.

She must carry out her plan or she would never have another chance.

She glanced sideways at Douglas. He was standing with his hands in his pockets watching them go, smiling to himself. Noticing her looking at him, he turned to face her.

"Well, I'm sure Milka has some more of that delicious coffee!" he said, cheerfully. "Shall I get you some, too?"

"Thank you, that would be very nice," replied Ruth. She sat on the veranda while he went inside, calling out for Milka.

Ruth looked out across the jewel-green treetops and past them to the blue hills. Automatically her eyes scanned for clouds, but there was nothing but dry, blue sky. It was relentlessly hot. She wondered if the rains would fall this year. *Please, God, bring the rain,* she found herself praying. *Please, God, let Douglas say yes when I ask.* She knew she didn't have the kind of faith in God that Douglas spoke about; nor did she have the relationship with Jesus that he said was so important. But she felt that in the last few weeks she had at least come to believe in God's existence, and surely that allowed her to pray to Him. Surely God must listen. She couldn't face the rest of her life alone; surely He understood that.

Douglas came with two steaming cups of coffee and set one down beside her.

"Well," he said, sitting down in the chair next to hers, "I think that was the most beautiful wedding I have ever attended in my life."

"It is the only wedding I have attended," Ruth said quietly, "but I know it was the most beautiful I'll ever see."

Douglas looked over at her and smiled his twinkling blue smile and melted Ruth's heart once again.

"I hope it won't take them long to settle in Uganda. There's some fine farming country there. I expect there will be a lot that I can do there, too. It must have been God's plan for me all along, if only I had listened to Him more carefully."

Douglas chatted on about where he was going to try to establish his hospital in Uganda. He already had plans to look along the shores of Lake Victoria. He was very enthusiastic. Ruth nodded politely whenever he paused, but she hardly heard a word he said.

At last, he looked at her and said, "I'm awfully sorry. I must be boring you to death with all my plans."

"No, no, not at all," Ruth replied, but they sat in silence for a moment. It was not their usual comfortable silence, and Douglas noticed.

"What's on your mind, Ruth? You look as though you're a million miles away. Is it Annie and Jimmy?"

This was her moment and she had to take it now. She took a long breath and closed her eyes for a silent, desperate prayer.

"Douglas, I have a proposition to make to you," she began slowly and deliberately.

Douglas laughed. "Well, when a woman tells me she has a proposition, I usually make for the hills, but since it's you, I won't."

Ruth didn't laugh. This was not an auspicious start. She decided to take the bull by the horns. "Douglas, you have made it quite clear that you are a confirmed bachelor." She noticed a shake in her voice, and she took another deep breath. She could see Douglas's face become concentrated and serious.

"Yes, I am," he said firmly and quietly. Ruth's stomach sank like a stone. But she had begun now, and there was only one way to go on.

"As you may have noticed, I am not the marrying kind, either." Douglas's face relaxed slightly. "Nevertheless," she went on bravely, "I have an idea that may be of benefit to both of us. I am hoping we might come to an arrangement." She began to talk faster. Douglas was ominously quiet.

"I have something you need, and you have something I would very much like to have. Since my father's death I have discovered that I own the piece of land next to the railway station. I cannot sell it to you because of the first refusal rights that the Campbells have over it. This brings me to my proposal. We could form a partnership, but in order for it to work, you and I would need to be married." Douglas still said nothing, so she rushed on.

"Of course, I understand that you would not like to limit your freedom with the responsibilities of marriage, and I am not proposing the kind of marriage where you will be limited in any way to your home base. I have been alone all my life, and I know how to look after myself." Ruth hardly paused for breath. "It would actually be to your advantage, since you do not intend to marry anyone anyway, to have this kind of arrangement with me because I would be willing to provide the bookkeeping and accounting for you as a partner, and you would therefore be free to practice medicine without all the administrative worry that you would otherwise be burdened with." She stopped talking at last, suddenly, and sat breathing hard, looking into her empty mug, afraid to look at Douglas.

Mercifully, Milka chose this moment to arrive with fresh coffee. They sat in silence until she went away. But Ruth glanced quickly at Douglas's face and knew she was lost.

"And what would the advantage of this arrangement be to you?" Douglas asked. His voice was quiet, and Ruth thought she detected a note of anger. Icy fingers gripped her heart, but she had to plunge ahead.

"You have something that I cannot seem to get hold of myself." She coughed. Her throat was constricting. She cleared it again. Douglas waited. "You have a life, and that is all I want. A life to call my own. Away from this farm."

"But you have a life. I don't know many women who would be able to run a farm in the middle of Africa single-handedly."

"Not many women would be able to stand being alone like I am. I have no one but me. I have nowhere to go and nothing else I can do. I am alone up here, and if I don't marry you, I will be alone up here for the rest of my life. I am good at farming, but I would never have chosen it myself. I would have been a nurse if I had a choice. It is too late for that now, but I can do bookkeeping and help with the nursing. In return for my land, you would give me the chance to do something I have chosen for myself. I think it is a fair bargain." She spoke with every last ounce of conviction she could muster. But Douglas's face was hard and inscrutable.

She looked down at her empty coffee mug again. She had done all she could. She spoke to God silently. The rest was now up to Him.

"Ruth." Ruth looked up in surprise. Douglas's voice was gentle and kind. "Ruth, I am sorry but I could never enter into that kind of a marriage. It is more of a business arrangement than a marriage. It wouldn't be fair to you, and it would be utterly despicable of me to marry you for your land." Ruth's throat tightened like it had a noose around it.

She cleared it again. "Douglas." She forced herself to be firm, but she knew it was a lost cause. "I need your hospital. I need it so I won't be tied forever to this farm. You say that God told you that Campbellburgh was the place for your hospital, and now I am offering you a way of letting it happen. Why are you not taking me up on it? There are no disadvantages for either of us. You are not planning to marry anyway, and no one will marry me. We could make a good partnership out of this."

"Ruth," Douglas leaned forward and looked intently into her face, "would you intend for us to be truly married? The way Annie and Jimmy are, for instance?"

Ruth blushed down to the tips of her toes. She had not intended to have to answer this kind of a question. She tried to open her mouth to speak, but she found it was impossible. She wanted with all her heart to say yes, but she couldn't possibly bring herself to actually utter the word. She riveted her eyes on the gold pattern on the edge of her cup. She could feel Douglas's eyes on her.

There was a long silence, and Douglas didn't move, and she couldn't look at him. Finally she found a last vestige of courage. "I always wanted to have children." She said it quietly and without looking up. Douglas leaned back in his chair and let out a long sigh. Ruth knew the worst was coming. She steeled herself.

"Ruth, I could never marry you. You deserve more than a business arrangement. You are right, you do deserve a life of your own, and you need someone who will truly be able to share it with you. I would be a poor excuse for a husband. I know you are upset with me for turning you down, but believe me, you will be happy one day. You will find someone much better than me, and you will be happier than you ever would have been with me.

"If you devote your life to loving God, as I have explained to you, He won't let you down. He came so that we could have life and have it abundantly. I am so sorry, Ruth, but it's for the best. It truly is."

Ruth looked up at him at last. Her eyes were dry and she found herself surprisingly calm. It was over now. She had done all she could and she had failed. She wished Douglas wouldn't bring God into it. God had done nothing to help her. But she smiled and his face betrayed a glimmer of relief.

"Well," she forced her voice to be strong and clear, "I hope I haven't embarrassed you. I felt I had to at least try all I could do. Let's put it behind us, shall we?" She smiled bravely into his face, expecting more of the relief she had just seen there, but his eyes were filled with pain.

"Believe me, Ruth, it's for the best." He looked almost desperate that she understand. But Ruth was not in the mood to help him with his pain. She was just starting out on a lifetime on her own, and she needed to preserve her strength.

There was another half hour before Annie and Jimmy would be back, and Ruth now decided it was going to be the longest half hour she had ever lived through. They sat together in silence, both grimly staring out onto the dry, dry valley.

"I hope the rains don't fail this year," said Ruth at last.

"Yes," Douglas replied, his voice quiet and almost sad. "Perhaps the wind will change soon."

"Oh, I hope it will." Ruth's voice had an unexpected note of desperation in it, and she fell silent.

A long silence later, she made out the figures of Annie and Jimmy returning up the dusty road. As they got closer, Ruth could feel their happiness radiating around them like a bright halo. In its center they moved and talked, blissfully unaware of the strained, unnatural silence between Ruth and Douglas.

It was time to go. Ruth looked at her friend and wondered when she would ever see her again. Annie reached out to Ruth and hugged her.

"Oh, Ruth, I'll miss you with all my heart. You've been the best friend I've ever, ever had. I wish you could be as happy as I am now. I will pray for you, Ruth."

"Good-bye, Annie." Her tears were falling. "Please write and tell me where you are. I'll miss you."

"Good-bye, my dearest friend." Annie hugged her more

tightly. She was crying, too.

"Thank you for everything, Ruth." Jimmy came over and Annie turned away from Ruth while he helped her into the car. "You have been a true friend." Jimmy put his hand out to Ruth and she shook it. Then, overcome with emotion, he drew her to him and hugged her good-bye.

Ruth was too filled with tears to reply.

Douglas climbed into the driver's seat and tipped his hat to Ruth. He opened his mouth to say good-bye, but suddenly he turned away from her and the engine roared. They started off with a jerk. Ruth stood waving, the tears running down her face.

"Annie, my friend," Ruth said as they drove away, "you are so lucky. I wish I were in your place, even as difficult as it is. My road leads into an endless, relentless desert, but yours will be filled with joy and love. You are so lucky." She paused, watching the plume of dust rise up behind them. "Good-bye Douglas," she said to the disappearing car, and turned to go inside. An iron chain of loneliness wrapped itself around her heart.

ten

The next few days trickled slowly by like streams at the end of the dry season, a mere shadow of the proud rivers that had bounded down the hillsides earlier. The farm life seemed dry and small. Even looking after the children who came for clinic in the mornings had shrunk to a small mechanical gesture for Ruth. She had put away her green dress in the old carved chest in the lounge, and already it smelled like mothballs, like a widow's wedding dress, the fading shell of a memory of love.

She tried not to think of Douglas or Annie and Jimmy. All that was a lifetime ago, and everyone was a million miles away now. And anyway, the rains were late, and Ruth had enough to worry about. She kept scanning the horizon for clouds, but the sky was hot and clear and as dry as the cracked riverbeds. Ruth felt her life trickling away into the dust.

Milka fussed over her, making her cups of tea at every opportunity and speaking cheerfully and enthusiastically about every little piece of news. She hadn't heard any news of Annie and Jimmy, and that was a good sign; they must have escaped. Ruth found herself saying a prayer for them now and then, before reminding herself that she didn't believe anymore. She could sense bitterness trying to grow in her heart like some unnatural thing that didn't need water or sunshine.

One day, she had to go into town to see Mr. Cooper to sign some papers to transfer the deed of ownership of the farm from her father's name into hers. Riding down into the valley, she realized that today she would be the sole owner of a farm in Africa. She, Ruth Morag Jones, a landowner and farmer in her own right. It was not the life she would have chosen, but nevertheless it was her own life now, and she had the power of control over it. She could retreat into a shell and subsist, or she could throw herself into it and at least lose herself in the work. And there would be some compensation. After all, while she would be alone, she would also be independent. Just like her father. She smiled ruefully to herself.

Riding out from under the canopy of the trees and into the searing heat of the hot, flat valley floor, she headed for the lone baobab tree in the distance, standing gnarled and proud out on the empty plain. Ruth smiled as she drew closer. The ancient tree greeted her like an old friend. The little flock of guinea fowl that lived in the shady grass nearby cackled and scuttled away as her horse approached, scolding and teasing her the way only those who know each other well can. And looking up into the branches of the tree, she thought she sensed a change in the wind. A breeze, like the forerunner of something new, slipped by overhead, rustling quickly through the dry leaves, and then it was gone.

Ruth sat straighter in her saddle. She would celebrate her new status by going to the hotel for lunch after she had seen Mr. Cooper. She would be dining alone, but she would hold her head high. The bitterness in her heart shrank a little.

A new thought moved into her mind: I now know the feeling of life. Just asking Douglas to marry her had made her feel alive if only for a few moments. And pain and tears were part of being alive. Even if God wouldn't listen to her prayers, even if she only barely believed in Him, she decided that she would at least be thankful for the little life she had. It was her own—she hadn't realized that until now. At that moment her bitterness shrank and shriveled away.

It seemed oddly quiet in town as she rode in. Without Douglas and Jimmy and Annie, the life had gone out of the place. Even the people on the streets looked quiet and subdued. Jimmy and Annie and Douglas will be bringing life and love and adventure to the people at their new towns, just as they had brought it here to her. But she would remember the lesson she had learned from them and thank God. Ruth smiled a friendly greeting to the people she recognized on the street, and they greeted her in return, a little surprised, she thought.

She conducted her business with Mr. Cooper efficiently and quickly. It's funny, she thought to herself, he doesn't seem quite such an enormous man anymore. Maybe Mabel has put him on a diet. On the other hand, perhaps it's just that I'm not so afraid anymore.

"Have you spoken to your Aunt Florence, lately?" he asked as he stood up to usher her to the door.

Ruth laughed a little sheepishly. "I'm afraid my aunt doesn't speak to me anymore."

"Oh, I'm sorry to hear that. I don't mean to intrude, but frankly, I'm a bit concerned about her. You have heard that Miss Campbell has eloped with young Jimmy MacRae?" Ruth nodded. "Well, naturally she is quite upset, but I'm afraid she hasn't seemed to be quite well, and I fear she is very much under the influence of Alex Kendall. I only hope everything will turn out for the best."

"I hope so, too," agreed Ruth. She put out her hand. "Thank you for your concern, Mr. Cooper. Perhaps it's time I tried to mend some fences with my aunt. I'll see what I can do."

Ruth left his office and headed for the hotel. She really did feel sorry for Aunt Florence, despite her unkind behavior. I'll call in to see her on my way out of town, she decided; but she would fortify herself with a good lunch before facing up to her.

It was a little sad riding up the driveway of the hotel, knowing that Douglas wasn't there anymore. The little thrill of joy with the hope of seeing him was gone, and there was a lonely, empty place in Ruth's heart now. But she set her face like flint. She was alone, and she was going to get used to it. She tied Chui up next to a large black car that looked suspiciously like Alex Kendall's friends' car, which she had seen before her father's funeral. Looking up into the dining room window, Ruth saw them sitting at a table where they could see all the comings and goings from the hotel. She wondered what they wanted. She hoped that Aunt Florence hadn't somehow gotten involved with them.

Like the town, the dining room seemed empty and quiet. But the food was still delicious.

It was just after her main course that Ruth noticed Alex Kendall's two friends stand up and look out of the window. There was a flurry of activity in the lobby, and the other diners stopped eating to watch. Suddenly, waiters began to rush about here and there, moving tables and chairs. Ruth put her knife and fork down and tried to figure out what was happening.

There was a flutter and a flurry of pink gauze and into the dining room burst Florence Campbell, dressed from head to toe in pink and carrying a huge bouquet of pink roses. Ruth stared in blank confusion. Alex Kendall appeared behind her. A small throng of admirers, including the reverend and Mrs. Montgomery, were following them closely. Florence and Alex swept over to the tables that had been rearranged just moments before.

The waiters settled them at their table and the entourage at the tables around them. Ruth noticed that the two men were now standing at the doors, almost like sentries. She could tell Alex was aware of them. He kept glancing in their direction, but they gave no indication that they noticed him.

A few minutes later, Florence rose majestically from her seat and cleared her throat. There was immediate silence.

"Ladies and gentlemen," she began in a regal tone, "as you all know, I have suffered a great deal in the last several months, what with losing my dear husband Angus, after having nursed him myself through a long and difficult illness. And now I find that I am suffering another deep and painful loss as my daughter, Annie, has, despite all my desperate attempts to help her make a good match, run away with a local farmer and married him. It has been a terrible trial to me, almost more than I can bear, but in the last few weeks I have been sustained by the care and, yes, even the love of this good and kind man, Alex Kendall." She turned to Alex and he stood up beside her.

"I am happy to announce to you all, my friends and relations, who know how much I have suffered and have tried to do your part to give me hope throughout it all, that I have found true happiness at last!

"Alex Kendall and I were married this morning in a quiet ceremony at the church, and we now ask all of you to join with me in celebrating our joyful union." There was a ghastly hush from the entire crowd. Ruth gasped out loud.

Gradually, as the news sank in, the crowd from the dining room began to buzz. Dutifully, people began to step forward to offer the bride and groom their congratulations. Alex was busy keeping one eye on the two sentries at the door, and Florence was wrapped up in a flurry of hugs and kisses and pink gauze and roses.

People filed back to their seats, and the waiters brought out bottles of champagne and glasses and distributed them to all the tables. A gentleman seated next to Florence, one of the poorer Campbells and a neighbor of Florence's, stood up.

"Ladies and gentlemen, I would like to propose a toast to the bride. There was a scraping of chairs and glasses everywhere clinked as the stunned diners all murmured, "To the bride."

Ruth stayed seated and left her glass of champagne untouched. The crowd, now over their initial surprise, buzzed with the excitement. Florence beamed brightly and Alex watched his two guards cautiously, as the waiters rushed around serving the wedding party lunch.

At last, as the diners began to filter out, returning to work and their daily lives, the room grew quieter. Florence began to gather her bouquet and got ready to leave. Alex grew visibly nervous. He glanced up at the sentries by the door. They were watching him. Ruth saw Alex look over at Florence. She was talking to the head waiter and had her back to him. Ruth could almost see him physically gathering his courage. He marched determinedly over to the two men and engaged them in intense conversation. At least Alex was intense, gesturing angrily and frowning, but the men simply shook their heads.

Alex turned and marched back to Florence. He drew her aside and whispered something in her ear. She went and talked with her new husband behind a stand of potted palms. Ruth saw her turn white and glance at the men by the door. They smiled thin, evil smiles at her. She looked pale and stunned, but nevertheless she took Alex by the arm and led him over to the far side of the dining room. He was cowering like a bad puppy.

Florence marched over to the two men. The sentries appeared grimly glad to see the effect they were having on the happy couple. They nodded as she approached them, but they didn't smile at her. She spoke to them sharply. The four of them sat together, and there was another intense discussion. Ruth watched fascinated. After a short while, Florence stood up and Alex and the two men followed suit. Florence grabbed Alex by the elbow and marched him out of the dining room. The two men sat, ordered more coffee and turned their chairs to watch the lobby. Alex and Florence burst into the manager's office, and a moment later he came scurrying out like a scalded cat. The door slammed behind him.

A warm breeze blew through the potted palms, and everyone looked a little calmer with Florence and Alex gone. Ruth paid her bill and slipped quietly down the flagstone steps into the garden. She wanted to think about this new development. She was stunned. How could Florence have married Alex Kendall, of all people? He must be at least ten, if not twenty years younger than she was. What on earth could have possessed her to do such a thing?

The sun burned itself into the hills behind her, as it had often been doing these days on her drives back to the farm. The old baobab stood glowing goldly with its shadow stretched out thinly behind it. It looked so much more lonely in the afternoon shadows than it did at midday.

Yes, thought Ruth, *maybe that's why Florence had married Alex. Like me, Florence couldn't face being alone, and Alex had agreed to her proposal.* She sighed. *A woman like Florence knew how to attract a man, while I couldn't even buy one to save my life.*

I'll go and make my peace with Florence after she's settled, Ruth thought. It seemed so strange to think about Alex Kendall taking the place of Angus Campbell. Ruth shuddered. But who could put oneself in another's shoes? Florence had her own pain. And her own way of coping with it.

She started up the hill and thought, *I look up to the hills from whence my help cometh. It must be a quote from the Bible,* Ruth thought. *Milka must have mentioned it to me once. Well, if there is any help for me in the hills, that is where I am going to be for most of my life,* she thought wryly.

Ruth rode home. Remembering her new resolve, she thanked God for her farm and for her livelihood. Thinking of God reminded her of Annie and Jimmy and Douglas, and she missed them all more than she could have ever imagined was possible. For the first time since they had left, her eyes filled with tears. She dismounted in front of the veranda steps with tears pouring down her cheeks. Through her tears, Ruth, as she did every day, scanned the horizon for clouds. "Oh, God, please bring the rain," she spoke out loud. The words felt as though they had been wrenched out of the center of her heart. In the silence that remained, someone answered.

It's coming. Soon. She felt, rather than heard, the reply. God answered her prayer. She was no longer alone. He was here, too. And there in the dust and the darkness in front of the veranda, she opened her heart and prayed to Jesus.

"Lord Jesus, I believe." She knew she was no longer alone, and the tears streamed down her face once more. Tears of relief and tears of joy. She was home at last.

eleven

The week went by in a blur of activity for Ruth. Milka was overjoyed at her decision to believe. "I have prayed all your life for you, and the Good Lord has at last answered my prayers. May His name be praised!" Milka lifted her hands to the sky as she said this and Ruth laughed with joy. For the first time in her life, she understood the joy that Milka always told her about when she spoke of her faith. Ruth had a million questions for Milka. Every afternoon while they drank tea together, she poured over the Bible at the kitchen table with her. It was a golden time.

Still the rains hadn't appeared, and the whole farm seemed to be holding its breath, waiting and waiting. But Ruth and Milka were busy in the house. Ruth pulled all her father's trophies off the walls. She covered the empty walls where the animal heads had been with her mother's pictures that she had brought with her from Scotland. Curtains were taken down and washed, floors were polished, and furniture was rearranged. Ruth took all the whiskey her father had kept in the sideboard and poured it out. She put china figurines and vases of wildflowers in place of the bottles and glasses. Light poured into the little farmhouse, and it was filled with the scent of flowers and fresh air. Ruth looked around her and again she thanked God.

There was only one discordant note that week. Kamau brought back news from town that Florence and Alex's marriage didn't appear to be going very well at all. Alex was living by himself at the hotel while Florence remained at home. There were rumors among the staff that the hotel was up for sale. Florence was at home and refused to see or speak to anyone. The whole town was buzzing with wild stories about what had made Florence marry Alex. In Kamau's opinion, she had run out of money on expensive nursing and cures, trying to save Angus's life.

Ruth felt deeply sorry for her aunt. She must have been suffering with fear and pain for a long, long time. She and Milka sat at the kitchen table the evening Kamau brought this news and prayed for Florence with all their hearts. Ruth thought she would try to go and see her aunt and apologize for her rude behavior toward her. She felt deep remorse for what she had said to her and prayed often that Florence would forgive her for being so unkind. But, even if she didn't, Ruth knew it would be good to show her that she had tried.

The next Sunday morning, Ruth left the farm in the buggy just at dawn. Ruth was on her way to church. Even the thought of the Reverend Montgomery's dull voice couldn't quench her enthusiasm for worshiping God. She was wearing her new green dress, and she felt as fresh and light as the leaves on the trees in the valley below.

Already the day promised to be hot. She strained her eyes, looking into the distance for a sign of the rains. She remembered the promise of rain that she had been given and wondered when it would be fulfilled. Her faith was so new to her, she wondered if perhaps she had made a mistake. But Milka assured her that waiting on God was something all Christians must learn, and she was already in the middle of her first lesson. She drove on through the forest, jiggling the horse's reins. She didn't want to be late for her first morning in church.

As Ruth passed by the elephant pool, the birds sang as sweetly in the slanting morning light that rippled through the leaves as they had the day the elephants had come to play. She remembered how far away and elusive joy and love had seemed to her then, as she clung to the tree watching the two elephants frolic together in the pool below her. And here she now possessed both love and joy. Truly God had already begun to speak to her then. He had spoken first. She bowed her head and whispered a prayer of thanksgiving to Him as she went by. The birds set it to music for her and sent it winging up to heaven.

Later, as she neared town and saw the roofs twinkling in the distance, she wondered how Florence was. She had half decided to stop in at the Campbell farm on the way back from church. Perhaps Florence would be at the service and she could get some sort of idea of what her condition was. Ruth had spent too many years suffering pain with Florence's sharp tongue to think about paying her a visit without a serious amount of trepidation. And she didn't yet really understand how Jesus could help her, but she had made up her mind that she would visit Florence soon.

Ruth arrived at church early, and there were only a few people trickling up the steps. The last time she had been here was at her father's funeral. So much had changed since then. She smiled warmly at the people going up the steps and received friendly greetings in response, although she could sense their surprise at seeing her here. She walked in the big wooden doors and stood for a moment, adjusting to the darkness inside. She wasn't sure where she should sit. Perhaps people had their own particular pews. She began to walk timidly up the aisle.

"Hello, Ruth!" Ruth recognized Constance Bishop, a friend of Annie's who was standing in front of the altar making last minute touches to the flower arrangements. She smiled. "Come and sit here at the front with me," Constance said, walking up to meet Ruth and taking her by the arm. "Jimmy told me all about what you did for Annie before he left. We are all so grateful to you. We have been praying for you and for Annie and Jimmy. Have you heard from them yet?"

"No, I haven't heard anything." She gratefully sat next to Constance.

Ruth and Constance's pew began to fill up, and Constance described Ruth's role in Annie's marriage to her friends. Ruth quickly found herself in the center of an admiring circle. "But, don't worry," whispered Constance to Ruth, "no one will tell Florence Campbell. She has enough troubles of her own these days anyway, poor, poor woman."

Ruth was worried. "What do you mean? What has happened?" But it was too late. The organ launched into the first hymn and the choir came walking down the aisle. As Ruth turned to look at them, someone caught her eye as he slipped quietly into the back pew. Surely it couldn't be Douglas MacPherson? She tried to catch another glimpse of the man, but he was directly behind her and hidden by several rows of people. It would be too impolite to turn around and crane her neck. It didn't matter anyway. She had probably just imagined someone else was Douglas, because she still thought of him so much. She quickly squashed the little flutter of anticipation that flared up whenever she thought she might see him.

She had a life of her own now, and she had Jesus to share it with her. She concentrated on the words of the hymn.

"Be Thou my vision. . ." the congregation sang, and with all her heart she sang, too.

After the service was over, she was again included in the conversation of her new friends. It was a strange feeling to be welcomed and spoken to by people she had hardly known, but it filled her heart with a peace and warmth that she truly had never thought possible. When Constance suddenly looked right past Ruth and waved to someone standing behind her, Ruth was completely taken by surprise to discover Douglas MacPherson standing there watching her. She had forgotten that she thought she had seen him earlier. The memory of their last meeting made her blush to the roots of her hair with embarrassment. She lowered her eyes and tried to avoid his gaze. Constance and the others were already crowding around him and asking for news of Annie and Jimmy.

Douglas explained that they had found some land and were in the process of putting up a house. Already Jimmy had decided that the crop he was going to try would be cotton. Annie was very happy, though she was anxious for news of her mother. As soon as he mentioned Florence, there was a sudden uncomfortable silence.

"What about your hospital?" someone asked. "Have you found the right location yet?"

Douglas paused and shot a quick glance at Ruth. She looked down to her shoes again and decided that she would slip out and fly away home. She only wanted to know that Annie was all right. Douglas's plans were too painful a subject for her to discuss objectively just yet.

"I haven't quite decided on anywhere just yet," she heard him explaining as she tiptoed down the church path, hoping no one would notice. "But I was called back to town on some urgent business."

Ruth didn't want to hear another word. She hoped his business wouldn't keep him long. She unhitched Chui and was just about to jump up into the buggy when someone took her by the waist and lifted her up. She caught her breath.

"Douglas!" She knew who it was before she looked.

"Lucky I caught you trying to sneak away!" He spoke with a tease in his tone of voice, but the softer look in his eyes betrayed that he understood why Ruth was running quickly away.

"Listen, Ruth," he said when she didn't smile, "I need to talk to you about something. Please come and have lunch with me at the hotel."

"Oh no, Douglas, I couldn't possibly do that. Really, I made a terrible fool of myself the other day. I can't imagine what came over me, but everything is different now." Ruth spoke as quickly as she could, trying to get away before he could persuade her otherwise. "Please do me the favor of completely forgetting we ever had that conversation. That would truly be the nicest thing you could do for me. I must go now. It was very nice to see you again, good-bye!" Ruth spoke desperately.

She couldn't face listening to his plans after the way she had tried to change them. She would have liked to tell him about her new faith in Jesus. After all, he had a lot to do with it, but the whole conversation would be too difficult. However, he had already thought of that angle and was using it to his advantage.

"All right then." He had a sly twinkle in his eyes. "If you won't listen to what I have to say, at least come with me and tell me what you are doing here in church this Sunday. I think you owe me an explanation of that, since I have told you all about my faith, not to mention encouraging you to have your own." He smiled up into her face, and Ruth's resolve evaporated. The only person to whom she had told the story of her faith in Jesus was Milka, and the need to tell someone, especially Douglas, was too much to resist. She slid over on the seat, and he hopped up onto the buggy beside her.

Ruth was surprised when they reached the hotel. All the staff greeted Douglas by name, and he and Ruth were immediately seated at the nicest table in the dining room. Douglas asked her to tell him the story of what brought her to church, and all through lunch they chatted about Ruth's new faith.

Ruth was touched because Douglas seemed particularly excited about it.

"From the day I set eyes on you at Angus Campbell's funeral, I have been praying for you," he said. "I sensed that the Lord had His hand on you and was searching for you."

"Searching for me!" Ruth said in surprise. "It was me who was searching for Him!" But they both laughed together. "No, you're right, it was He who made the first move," she said, remembering the elephants at the pool. As she looked at Douglas laughing with her across the table, she knew that everything was the same again between them. They were friends. Just for a moment, she felt a pang of regret, wishing there was more than friendship, but instead, she remembered to thank God for restoring her friendship with Douglas. No one could want a nicer friend than him.

As they finished their lunch and the waiter brought coffee, Douglas became serious. "Ruth," he said, "there is something I want to tell you about me."

Ruth had a sudden fear that he was going to bring up the subject of her proposal. "No," she said firmly, "let's just be friends as we are. You don't need to discuss anything else with me!"

"Ruth, stop!" Douglas interrupted. "Stop and listen to me. I need to explain something to you if we are to be friends. It is important to me."

Ruth sat silently. She steeled herself against the thought of being embarrassed by the mention of her proposal. But she needn't have worried.

"A long time ago," Douglas began, "when I was just starting my medical studies, I was in love with a young girl from my hometown in Alberta. Her name was Jane. We were engaged to be married, but we had to wait until I had finished my studies in Toronto.

"Jane and I wrote back and forth to each other regularly.

She was looking forward to my return that summer. But in the spring, my cousin Alex returned from the Klondike, where he had been looking for gold. He hadn't found much, or if he had, he had already spent it on gambling.

"Anyway, the long and the short of it is that when I returned to Alberta that summer, it didn't take me long to figure out that Alex was trying to steal Jane away from me. I was terribly upset, and I lost my temper with Alex, said terrible things to him, and we got into a fistfight. I am ashamed to say it was in front of Jane. Jane was horrified at my behavior, and I can't say I blame her. I behaved very badly. She dropped me like a hot potato and began to see Alex. She seemed very happy, and by the end of the summer, when I went back to Toronto, she and Alex were engaged to be married.

"I threw myself into my studies and tried not to think about what had happened that summer. At Christmastime I received a letter from my mother explaining that Jane was expecting a baby and that Alex had left town. If I was angry with Alex before, I was beside myself with anger now!" Douglas paused and took a deep breath.

"Anyway, I wrote to Jane and offered to come home and marry her. Now that I look back on it, I must have seemed awfully arrogant to Jane. Although I wrote several letters, I never heard back from her.

"The following summer, when I went back to work on the farm, I discovered that Jane had married a local boy, and she had had her baby. Her new husband was a poor farm worker and they didn't have much. But her baby had a name. She wouldn't speak to me and avoided me whenever she could.

"Each summer that I came home, Jane had another baby, and she was poorer than ever. There were rumors that her husband drank and beat her. But still, she wouldn't even look at me if I passed her in the street.

"Finally, when I was studying in seminary to prepare for

the mission field, I heard from Mother that Jane had died. The story was that her husband had come home one night, having had too much to drink, and beaten her. She was expecting another baby, and with the beating, the baby came too soon and there were complications. Both Jane and the child died. The other children were put up for adoption, and I heard no more.

"But I thought about it all the time. I vowed to never allow myself to go through that kind of pain again. I decided that I was called to be single, and anyway, taking a wife and family into the mission field would be too difficult. I had made a decision and I put the matter of marriage behind me. But I had never put the matter of Alex behind me. I was furious with him. Of course, a good missionary doesn't go around being angry with people, so gradually after several years my anger grew cold and hard. It didn't go anywhere, it just took on a different, more manageable shape.

"When I was home and saw Alex at family gatherings, I was polite and formal, just the way a good Christian ought to behave, so I thought. Alex began to take an interest in my goal of going to Africa. He had heard that there was money to be made in Africa, and Alex always had an ear for money-making schemes, although he never stuck with any of them long enough to actually get rich.

"Last year, when my father died and I inherited my share of the estate, Alex tried to persuade me to go into the safari business with him. He said it was the new age of tourist travel and we would double our money in five years. Of course, I ignored him and came here to build my hospital. But, as you know, he followed me. He tried to talk me into his schemes when we were staying at the lodge. What I didn't know at the time was that he had racked up huge gambling debts, and he needed a way to pay them back. When I wasn't helpful to him, he decided to marry Annie and at least use some of her money to pay off his debts. But there wasn't a lot of time because, as you know, the people he owed money to tracked him here and were demanding it soon.

"So when Annie eloped with Jimmy, it put him in a very difficult position. He turned to Florence, not realizing that Florence had also been counting on his marriage to Annie for entirely different reasons. Florence had spent all her money and mortgaged the hotel to the roof trying to find a cure for her husband's illness. She thought that, like me, Alex had family money, and she would be able to use it to get herself out of debt once he was her son-in-law.

"You know the rest of the story. Alex sent me a telegram last week asking for help. I was about to give him my usual response when I realized that God forgave me my sins, but I refused to forgive Alex his. I was overcome with remorse for all the years I had played the holier-than-thou Christian with Alex, and I wired him the money he needed. We are also going into the tourism business together. I paid the back payments on the hotel's mortgage, and Alex will run the hotel and try to make some honest money. I have enough left to start my hospital in Uganda, and with God's help, we will make a little from the hotel to finish off the hospital."

Ruth and Douglas sat together in silence for a few minutes while Ruth absorbed all this news.

"What about Florence?" she asked at last. "Are she and Alex going to make a go of their marriage?"

"That's one thing I can't tell you," Douglas replied. "I don't honestly know how a marriage can work when it began under such a cloud of deception. But, I suppose we'll just have to wait and see."

Ruth sighed. "Why did you tell me all this?"

"I wanted you to know. I know our last meeting was difficult, but I hope with all my heart that we can still be friends. I would like it very much if we could."

Ruth couldn't bring herself to look at him. She put her elbows on the table and put her face in her hands. Perhaps they had gone too far together, and now they couldn't go back to just being friends after all. "Douglas, I don't know," she heard herself say. "I thought we could, but now I feel perhaps I was wrong."

Douglas scraped his chair backward and stood up. He walked around and took Ruth's arm as she stood up, too. "Look, Ruth," he said quietly, "I'm sure it has been a long day for you, and it's getting late. Why don't you think about it? Would it be all right if I came to see you the day after tomorrow, before I go back to Uganda? If you think we can no longer be friends, just send me word here at the hotel and I won't come."

"Okay," Ruth replied, glad to have a way out for a day or two. "Bye, Douglas." She turned and fled from the dining room aware that his eyes were on her all the way.

It was with a full heart that she drove back out of town and up the hillside to her farm. The old baobab tree standing alone on the plain with its little flock of guinea fowl nodded a friendly greeting in the wind, and Ruth was sure she sensed a change in the air. Surely it wouldn't be long now before the rains came.

twelve

Ruth spent the next day immersed in prayer and thought. She knew that somehow she would have to find a way of controlling her powerful feelings for Douglas. She simply couldn't let him go without being his friend. She would regret it for the rest of her life, so she didn't send him word not to come. On the day she expected him, she dressed in her green dress and carefully brushed her hair, but her hands were shaking with nervous anticipation. She prayed for strength and peace. She wanted with all her strength to be bright and happy and friendly when he came, but it was nearly impossible. She had no peace. Perhaps it was a mistake, she thought as she saw Rosie's cloud of dust rising above the brow of the hill, but it was too late now.

Douglas pulled Rosie up to the veranda steps and jumped out. Ruth was surprised to see him wearing a suit and tie, with his hair firmly brushed down. But instead of his usual breezy hello, he took Ruth by the hand. "You look beautiful today," he said.

"Hello, Douglas," replied Ruth carefully. There was a moment of awkward silence as they stood at the top of the veranda. Ruth turned to lead the way inside.

"Listen, Ruth," Douglas spoke quickly, "how about a walk before we have tea? I thought it might be nice to walk back down to that spot where Annie and Jimmy were married. It is so beautiful down there, I'd really like to see it again."

"Well, don't you think we're a bit overdressed to go tramping through the bush?" It was now Ruth's turn to speak nervously. That place meant so much to her, and all her memories and feelings would be so close to the surface there. But she had been taken off her guard and she couldn't come up with a way to say no.

"Come on," he said, opening Rosie's door for her, "let's drive down the hill."

Why would Douglas get himself all dressed in a tie and leather shoes just to traipse down into the bottom of a jungle path with me? He is really a very baffling man, she thought as they drove together in silence.

When they reached the little glade by the pool, Douglas stood beside her as she stopped and looked into the water. The pool itself seemed to be holding its breath, waiting for the rain. The water that fell into it from the stream was a faint trickle, and the ring of dried mud that surrounded the pond looked thirsty and parched. There was complete silence. Not even a bird twittered in the trees above them. The whole place seemed to be waiting nervously. Ruth could feel Douglas's presence beside her in the quiet more intensely than she had ever felt him before. She held her breath.

"Ruth," Douglas broke the silence. His voice was low and quiet, as though he were afraid of his own words. "Ruth, I need to apologize to you for something."

"No, I'm sure you don't." Ruth spoke quickly, suddenly embarrassed.

"Please listen to me, Ruth. I must speak to you about this." Douglas was firm and Ruth listened. "Remember our conversation on Annie and Jimmy's wedding day? I haven't been able to get it out of my mind." He paused to see that Ruth understood what he was referring to.

She was horrified. She could hardly believe Douglas would actually bring up such a painful subject.

"Douglas, it was nothing," she said desperately. "Please forget about it. And you owe me no apology. If that is all you came to discuss, please don't. I would rather we left now." She turned to go.

"Ruth!" He took hold of her arm to stop her from walking away from him, and she looked up into his eyes. "Ruth, I have made a terrible mistake. When I told you that I never planned to marry, it was not because that was God's will for my life, rather it was out of bitterness and unforgiveness. It was wrong of me." He paused and took a deep breath.

"Ruth, I want to ask you to marry me. I love you."

Ruth felt a warm breeze blow around her. She felt there was nothing else in all the world but Douglas and her and the soft, warm wind blowing around them. She closed her eyes, and his words continued to flood over her.

"Ruth," he said, "I've been a fool. I have loved you since the day I met you, and I should never have let you have to ask me to marry you. I should have asked you long before it came to that. And to think you felt you had to offer me your land. How could I let the woman I love think I married her for her land? I am so sorry." He reached forward and took her two hands in his. His voice was a whisper now. "Ruth, I love you. Please marry me."

Ruth couldn't answer. All she could do was smile up into his face through the tears that were falling like rain down her cheeks. She felt his hands let go of hers, and he put his arms around her and drew her to him and kissed her. He kissed her mouth and her cheeks and her eyes and her neck, until she was completely immersed in his love for her. And she kissed him back.

A long time later, the wind began to blow strongly and insistently. Douglas and Ruth held each other closer, and then rain began to fall. As the drops splashed down on them and around them, they drew apart. The rumbling in the distance that they had been only dimly aware of a few minutes before was suddenly shaking the earth under them and rattling the trees around them. Flashes of lightning tore through the sky.

"I think we'd better go up to the car quickly," Douglas said in a hoarse, intimate voice Ruth had never heard before. He put his arm around her waist and led her up the hillside.

Lightning flashed around them, and Ruth was terrified. Douglas pulled her closer to him, and they scrambled quickly up the path. Finally, they came to Rosie. Douglas lunged for the door and threw Ruth inside and himself after her. They sat for a few moments listening to the rain drumming onto the roof and streaming down the windows around them. Then Douglas got out and turned the crank, starting Rosie up with a welcoming roar. Slowly, they made their way up the hill. When they came to the house, they made a dash for the door and stood dripping and laughing together on the threshold.

Milka came running in to greet them and gave a shriek of delight when she saw Douglas. "*Bwana* Douglas, I knew you would be back! I knew it. Praise be to our Lord! Let me get you some tea."

She bustled off in a flurry of excitement, and Ruth found Douglas some dry clothes. She looked ruefully at his mud-coated leather shoes and his soaked white shirt and shook her head.

"Well," he spoke sheepishly, as he took the dry clothes, "I wanted to make a good impression on you."

"You did that a long time ago." She looked down shyly at the floor.

And a few minutes later, they were dry and cozy, sitting together in the dining room sipping tea, with Milka peeping around the corner every two minutes to make sure Douglas hadn't left.

Douglas looked around at the light, cheerful room. "My, you've changed things since I was here last!"

Ruth laughed. "Yes, everything has changed since you

were here last! I have changed."

"I'm not so sure of that," Douglas replied. "It's more like you have become yourself now." He reached for her hand and kissed it.

Ruth reveled in her happiness. She could smell the damp earth outside, and she could almost feel the grass and the land drinking in the rain and filling up and growing green again. The storm was passing over now, and the sun was setting behind it. A shaft of red-gold light flashed into the room, and everything was as golden and glowing as Ruth felt in her heart.

A Letter To Our Readers

Dear Reader:

In order that we might better contribute to your reading enjoyment, we would appreciate your taking a few minutes to respond to the following questions. When completed, please return to the following:

Rebecca Germany, Managing Editor
Heartsong Presents
P.O. Box 719
Uhrichsville, Ohio 44683

1. Did you enjoy reading *The Promise of Rain?*
   ❑ Very much. I would like to see more books
      by this author!
   ❑ Moderately
      I would have enjoyed it more if _____
      _____

2. Are you a member of **Heartsong Presents**? ❑Yes ❑No
   If no, where did you purchase this book?_____
   _____

3. What influenced your decision to purchase this
   book? (Check those that apply.)

   ❑ Cover   ❑ Back cover copy

   ❑ Title   ❑ Friends

   ❑ Publicity   ❑ Other_____

4. How would you rate, on a scale from 1 (poor) to 5
   (superior), the cover design?_____

5. On a scale from 1 (poor) to 10 (superior), please rate the following elements.

___Heroine   ___Plot

___Hero   ___Inspirational theme

___Setting   ___Secondary characters

6. What settings would you like to see covered in **Heartsong Presents** books?_____

_____

_____

7. What are some inspirational themes you would like to see treated in future books?_____

_____

_____

8. Would you be interested in reading other **Heartsong Presents** titles?   ❏ Yes   ❏ No

9. Please check your age range:
   ❏ Under 18   ❏ 18-24   ❏ 25-34
   ❏ 35-45   ❏ 46-55   ❏ Over 55

10. How many hours per week do you read? _____

Name _____

Occupation _____

Address _____

City_____ State_____ Zip_____

......Hearts♥ng ......

HEARTSONG PRESENTS TITLES AVAILABLE NOW:

___HP 64 CROWS'-NESTS AND MIRRORS, *Colleen L. Reece*

___HP103 LOVE'S SHINING HOPE, *JoAnn A. Grote*

___HP111 A KINGDOM DIVIDED, *Tracie J. Peterson*

___HP112 CAPTIVES OF THE CANYON, *Colleen L. Reece*

___HP131 LOVE IN THE PRAIRIE WILDS, *Robin Chandler*

___HP132 LOST CREEK MISSION, *Cheryl Tenbrook*

___HP135 SIGN OF THE SPIRIT, *Kay Cornelius*

___HP140 ANGEL'S CAUSE, *Tracie J. Peterson*

___HP143 MORNING MOUNTAIN, *Peggy Darty*

___HP144 FLOWER OF THE WEST, *Colleen L. Reece*

___HP163 DREAMS OF GLORY, *Linda Herring*

___HP167 PRISCILLA HIRES A HUSBAND, *Loree Lough*

___HP168 LOVE SHALL COME AGAIN, *Birdie L. Etchison*

___HP175 JAMES'S JOY, *Cara McCormack*

___HP176 WHERE THERE IS HOPE, *Carolyn R. Scheidies*

___HP179 HER FATHER'S LOVE, *Nancy Lavo*

___HP180 FRIEND OF A FRIEND, *Jill Richardson*

___HP183 A NEW LOVE, *VeraLee Wiggins*

___HP184 THE HOPE THAT SINGS, *JoAnn A. Grote*

___HP187 FLOWER OF ALASKA, *Colleen L. Reece*

___HP188 AN UNCERTAIN HEART, *Andrea Boeshaar*

___HP191 SMALL BLESSINGS, *DeWanna Pace*

___HP192 FROM ASHES TO GLORY, *Bonnie L. Crank*

___HP195 COME AWAY MY LOVE, *Tracie J. Peterson*

___HP196 DREAMS FULFILLED, *Linda Herring*

___HP199 DAKOTA DECEMBER, *Lauraine Snelling*

___HP200 IF ONLY, *Tracie J. Peterson*

___HP203 AMPLE PORTIONS, *Dianne L. Christner*

___HP204 MEGAN'S CHOICE, *Rosey Dow*

___HP207 THE EAGLE AND THE LAMB, *Darlene Mindrup*

___HP208 LOVE'S TENDER PATH, *Birdie L. Etchison*

(If ordering from this page, please remember to include it with the order form.)

·········· Presents ··········

__HP211 MY VALENTINE, *Tracie J. Peterson*

__HP215 TULSA TRESPASS, *Norma Jean Lutz*

__HP216 BLACK HAWK'S FEATHER, *Carolyn R. Scheidies*

__HP219 A HEART FOR HOME, *Norene Morris*

__HP220 SONG OF THE DOVE, *Peggy Darty*

__HP223 THREADS OF LOVE, *Judith McCoy Miller*

__HP224 EDGE OF DESTINY, *Darlene Mindrup*

__HP227 BRIDGET'S BARGAIN, *Loree Lough*

__HP228 FALLING WATER VALLEY, *Mary Louise Colln*

__HP235 THE LADY ROSE, *Joyce Williams*

__HP236 VALIANT HEART, *Sally Laity*

__HP239 LOGAN'S LADY, *Tracie J. Peterson*

__HP240 THE SUN STILL SHINES, *Linda Ford*

__HP243 THE RISING SUN, *Darlene Mindrup*

__HP244 WOVEN THREADS, *Judith McCoy Miller*

__HP247 STRONG AS THE REDWOOD, *Kristin Billerbeck*

__HP248 RETURN TO TULSA, *Norma Jean Lutz*

__HP251 ESCAPE ON THE WIND, *Jane LaMunyon*

__HP252 ANNA'S HOPE, *Birdie L. Etchison*

__HP255 KATE TIES THE KNOT, *Loree Lough*

__HP256 THE PROMISE OF RAIN, *Sally Krueger*

Great Inspirational Romance at a Great Price!

Heartsong Presents books are inspirational romances in contemporary and historical settings, designed to give you an enjoyable, spirit-lifting reading experience. You can choose wonderfully written titles from some of today's best authors like Peggy Darty, Sally Laity, Tracie Peterson, Colleen L. Reece, Lauraine Snelling, and many others.

When ordering quantities less than twelve, above titles are $2.95 each. Not all titles may be available at time of order.

Hearts♥ng Presents
Love Stories Are Rated G!

That's for godly, gratifying, and of course, great! If you love a thrilling love story, but don't appreciate the sordidness of some popular paperback romances, **Heartsong Presents** is for you. In fact, **Heartsong Presents** is the *only inspirational romance book club*, the only one featuring love stories where Christian faith is the primary ingredient in a marriage relationship.

Sign up today to receive your first set of four, never before published Christian romances. Send no money now; you will receive a bill with the first shipment. You may cancel at any time without obligation, and if you aren't completely satisfied with any selection, you may return the books for an immediate refund!

Imagine. . .four new romances every four weeks—two historical, two contemporary—with men and women like you who long to meet the one God has chosen as the love of their lives. . .all for the low price of $9.97 postpaid.

To join, simply complete the coupon below and mail to the address provided. **Heartsong Presents** romances are rated G for another reason: They'll arrive *Godspeed!*
